Weird Waypoints: A Speculative Travel Guide to the Between

edited by Sarah Karasek

Weird Waypoints: A Speculative Travel Guide to the Between
ISBN: 979-8-218-25685-2

Contents

Introduction

by Sarah Karasek

The journey can be more exciting, more fun, and often scarier than the destination. These stories examine those side trips and pit stops, triumphs and pitfalls, encountered along the way.

I spent a year driving a three-hour commute, twice a week, to graduate school and back. At first it was hectic. It was intimidating. But as time went on, I got to know the gas station in Leesport, PA with the cleanest restrooms for 60 miles and the other gas station on the way back with the restroom that has the broken sink and the door that doesn't lock. I shielded my eyes twice a week for months at that sharp turn on the windy mountain road where the sun suddenly splashed across the windshield. And I praised the change in the positioning of the planet when I no longer had to shield my eyes.

Twice a week, I greeted the tall iron gates of the little cemetery along the shortcut that my GPS didn't know about. And I memorized all the pot holes along that stretch of highway where everyone drives at least ten miles over the seventy mile per hour speed limit – only for the pot holes to be filled and new holes to emerge every other week.

Two weeks before I no longer needed to drive to classes, I finally stopped at the Mexicon-Korean restaurant with the perpetually empty parking lot and ordered one of the best burritos I've ever eaten. I was the only customer, and a friendly waiter (who turned out to be the owner) told me I just happened to drive past between their lunch rush and their dinner rush, when people often needed to reserve tables.

The stories within these pages take mundane encounters like these, and often much more exciting ones, and tell them in weird, speculative, surreal ways – ranging from the beautifully ephemeral to the viserally horrifying. They celebrate travel and growth, explore the shadowy corners of tourism, and transport you into their own weird worlds.

I hope you enjoy the journey.

How to Map the Amusement Park You Keep Driving by in the Highways of Your Dreams

by M. Lopes da Silva

If you spend any amount of time driving or being transported along major roads or highways, you will start to drive the nightways when you dream. They look a lot like regular highways but the nightways are distinct: these roads drive through you.

Every nightway passes by a few roadside attractions. An arcana of ghost towns and gas stations and diners like postcards bleaching in the sun. At least one amusement park. If you haven't spotted it yet, keep driving. Look for the speckle of bright light in the dark; colors so stark the brain blips to contemplate them. Magenta magic, enigmatic and holy. Mystery colors – they dazzle!

Find the correct offramp to take. This might take a while, so be patient. Follow any signs you see: these are messages from yourself.

Sometimes the offramp will lead you to a parking lot, and sometimes you will glide effortlessly into the park, your vehicle always a ride, derailed and route-less, but with no instructions to keep your hands and arms inside you might lose a finger or something even more precious to you.

You find parking or you circle the lot and the circling is the exhilaration and the anxiety, a parent's temper boiling behind the steering wheel as restless legs fling little feet into seat cushions air vents stereo systems just about anywhere, really. The rubber from tiny sneakers skids sticky along the hard plastic and no one is really there yet. Nobody ever will be.

It's so exhausting to travel anywhere. Let the car collapse under your skin, iron returning to your blood. Passengers were pieces of you that converge now, puzzling together. Gasoline reverse engineers to power your metal dinosaur bones. Now you're trans-figured. An animatronic: a mascot, a star. Beloved and smothered and never seen. Nobody will know that you're queer. Nobody will see your discomfort. You will vigorously whip your neck around to make it look like the mascot's lips are moving when a recorded message plays from hidden speakers: "Welcome." If you don't find a way to get out, you will probably die in that suit smelling like somebody else's vomit.

If you hatch free of that foam and felt egg of non-being to find love of your own you will discover the entrance to the theme park. Where is it located? Write that down somewhere. This fact is important: you're making a map, after all. Make sure to remember where you parked.

The entrance is the thing that opens you. It is a key that looks like a door. Another name for this door is "love." It is not always a tunnel.

After the entrance is a landscape of desire. What do you want? Satisfy your small appetites: your money's no good here because everything is free.

The fairy tale gardens are gentle, kind, foam-padded so when you fall to your knees there will be no irreparable damage done. Color the outlines of the fae grounds emerald and lime and teal – neon hues that taste like the woods on your tongue.

The roller coasters scream your fears out loud to everyone so what can you do? What can you do? The machines will eject the contents of your guts by force, which will abruptly become everyone's problem all at once. My god. Submit to the mechanism's metal hubris and let it toss you around for a while – remember that the wait times are always much longer than the actual ride times – you will survive this, too. You always could.

The haunted house is always haunted, but never just by ghosts. The mascot's skin is waiting there for you, a shredded husk that wants you to wear it again.

Leave it behind. There is a reassurance in drawing the eyedrop and shuttlecock silhouettes of ghosts. Plenty of friendly wobbles to trace. Careful eyedrop centers.

The fun house's mirrors teach you that you are more than a shape. You transcend your own reflections. You always could.

The dark rides are the shadowy places where your other selves have all been stored. On wiggling tracks you can reiterate well-lit life-size dioramas of the past. Some of these rides are a joy to return to, others the kind of thing that makes your pulse race in your gullet, unbidden. Just remember, you don't have to go on every ride.

If there is a water flume, the thrill of what's next could float your log along bumping the seminal sub-liminal writhing curious waterways bursting finally down and up (caution: you may get wet) — but don't worry if you don't see one at your park.

The best place to see the fireworks is at the edge of the lake. Standing there someone you love is holding your hand. You are held and a star is exploding above you and you are a star exploding and holding yourself in your hand.

The skin of your old suit is moldering, growing shabbier and more uncomfortable to wear every second you spend free of its rotten polyester. A frozen, smiling mouth that never had anything to say at all is on display as it slowly falls apart, foam blistering, pinned to a steel frame that haunts only a very small section of an amusement park that barely exists, after all.

A map is a souvenir of where you were going, once. You can always get back in your car (if you remember where you parked), return to the artery of nightways, and keep driving. There's a diner a little way up the road that serves a decent cup of coffee and rhubarb pie. From there you can figure out where to go next.

Big Flo's All-American Roadkill Diner & Last Chance Bar and Grill Truck Stop for Normal Human Motorists

by Bitter Karella

3 ½ stars

Closed: Will reopen when the blood moon rises and the stars align.

Location: Take any wrong exit off the Interstate and drive.

When you take the "wrong exit off the Interstate" and find yourself on a "deserted dirt road that seemingly runs forever toward the horizon" but that "isn't on any map," be sure to stop in to Big Flo's for a "real slice of Americana." This "folksy," "down-home" eatery offers "suspiciously cheap wares," about which your waitress will only "smile wanly" when questioned, and "your deepest, darkest desires fulfilled – for a price." "Mysterious," "Harrowing," and "Definitely from an animal of some kind, I couldn't bring myself to ask" are some of the things diners have said about the Fried Liver 'n' Onions. Other "Can't Miss" dishes are the Animal Meat Sandwich, Indeterminate Fried Poultry, Grandma's Bone Cake and a "Soup from which the faces of those whom you have wronged stare accusingly." Flo's proudly serves two kinds of salad: "a ranch-doused head of iceberg lettuce that induces madness and despair" and "the same but with a hard-boiled egg on top." A "jukebox that always plays haunting, tuneless calliope music that portends unsettling events to come" has been described as "rustic" and "charming" by some.

Diners rave that "every sandwich comes with mayonnaise, even the ones that by all rights should have some other sauce." Be sure to ask your waitress "Does this have mayonnaise?" before ordering. She will "look at you like you're crazy" and "insist that of course it does not have mayo." You order it. It arrives. It has mayonnaise. The fries are "covered in big gobs of mayonnaise." The salad is "dressed with mayonnaise." As the waitress "tops" off your drink, "big viscous chunks of mayo plop from her pitcher into your glass." You run to "the bathroom." When you turn the taps on the sink, mayonnaise "leaks out" in a "steady stream of eggy slurry." You open your mouth, but your throat is "choked with mayonnaise" and all you can do is "scream silently" as a "vomitous spew of Hellman's Original pours from your lips."

Regulars recommend that you ask for "Flo's Secret Menu" and don't be put off by the "suddenly terrified waitress" insisting that "We're just a normal diner here! Just a normal diner!" or demanding to "know who told you about that." An extra tip of "two copper coins stolen from the eyes of a dead man" or "an image of a loved one burned in a brazier" may encourage better service. Diners describe watching their waitress eat the tip, exposing "cracked, blackened teeth" and "the fat gray tongue of a corpse," as "part of the experience." Adventurous eaters should order "Flo's Famous Burger," which is not just a "burger with mayonnaise on it that costs an extra $3, no, it's much more. Much, much more." When it arrives, remember to "eat it all, whatever it is" to "seal the pact." The bill, when it arrives, is described as "cryptic" and "written in some form of unearthly runes, the meaning of which will only gradually make sense with mounting horror." Be sure to "leave your cash and credit card at home," Flo's won't accept it. Your server will promise to "settle up at the end." Warning! If the waitress "offers to trade places with you," do not accept her offer. When you leave Flo's, "do not look back."

Some Trips Are Not Worth Remembering

by Corey Farrenkopf

A few miles down Route 28, you'll come to the first discount t-shirt shop, the ocean's lull humming in your ears. You've seen people in every part of the country wearing the shirts, the looping pastel scrawl of *Cape Cod* written on their chests, and you know that you, too, need one to prove that you were here, on this peninsula, alive for some period of time.

The building's facade is reminiscent of a dilapidated seaside cottage, white painted shingles and nautical baubles nailed to the wall. The architecture is fitting for what had once been an old fishing village, the buoys and anchors and clamming rakes strung along the siding. You push through the front door and are greeted with thousands and thousands of t-shirts, ranging in all colors of the spectrum, arrayed in winding, hip high, aisles.

There are dozens of other shoppers milling about, sifting through the shirts like they are vinyl at a record shop, searching for their size, their preferred pigment.

You take your place among the throng and sift for a medium maroon, but there are only larges and smalls, so you move to the next color, periwinkle, which isn't great with your complexion, but what can you do? This pile only contains XLs. The next pile, gray heather, is only smalls with a singular extra small at the bottom. You jostle your way through the cramped bodies, apologizing for the contact, the breach of personal space, digging and digging through the t-shirts, but there are no mediums. Not a single one.

You go to the cash register and inquire about their lack of fitting resort attire, whether there might be some more in storage. The young man at the desk with the slicked back red hair shrugs, barely looking up from the register as if the secrets of the world are written on the flashing green LCD display.

"You can always go next door. They have similar stock to satisfy similar desires," he says.

"There's another t-shirt shop?" you ask.

"Of course," the cashier responds. "You can't have just one in a place like this. So many wants. So many needs."

So you leave, drive out of the parking lot, and swing into the next lot where a nearly identical store, with a nearly identical facade, sits waiting for you. There's a plastic bass on the wall instead of an anchor, but otherwise, the difference is negligible.

As you get out of the car, you notice the sound of the ocean seems closer than before, the swell and crash of waves, seagull caw and undertow suck. You tell yourself it makes sense. You are surrounded by water even if you can't see it, even if all you see is squat businesses stretching out of sight down the road. The sea is always there, waiting just beyond the tree line.

You step into the second t-shirt shop and it is nearly identical to the first. The winding aisles of merchandise, the dozens and dozens of people bent over the stacks of clothing, searching and searching for their desired apparel. They too need to prove that they've been here, that at one point in their lives they had enough money for a vacation to the peninsula that everyone else supposedly visited. They have the shirts. They have the evidence. The rest of the world must accept their passage. There's no denying it.

The cashier looks almost the same as the one next store, but his hair is black and he's decently sunburned, skin flaking on his exposed forearms and neck. You try to wave, but the man doesn't look at you, attention fully absorbed by the register's electronic display, so you move off into the flow of customers, elbowing for a spot at the table to sort through maroon shirts once more.

But there are, once again, no mediums.

You make your way from one pile of shirts to the next, failing to find the right size. You think maybe you can still fit into a small, but you know that hasn't worked since you were in your mid-twenties, and that time has long passed. And a large won't do either. You'll swim in it, so you ask the woman next to you if she's spied a single medium in her own quest about the store. She looks up from her sorting, eyes half lidded as if partially in a dream, her gaze lingering off beyond your shoulder, ear tilted towards a sound you can't quite hear.

"Everyone wants the medium. What else would one desire?" she asks, before sinking her hands back into the pile of shirts, clawing through the hundred percent cotton heap.

"Other sizes maybe?" you reply.

The woman chuckles quietly to herself, shoulders rising and falling, fingers worming through cheap fabric. You step away from her, afraid there is something wrong. You've heard that even in vacationland there are drug problems, addiction rates on the rise, dark secrets lingering beneath the pristine postcard veneer. You don't know what she'll do for her desired shirt, the lengths she'll go. You know what you will do, but beyond that, others are a concerning mystery.

"The next shop might have what you seek. It's just down the road. You can't miss it," the cashier says once you ask the question once again.

"Isn't that a lot of competition for such a small place?" you ask.

"There's no competition when there's only one source that can satiate your desires. Go on. You will see."

The next shop is the same as the last and same as the first. The t-shirts exist in slightly different colors, most of them faded, dye almost bleeding. The fabric feels damp beneath your palms, the humidity of the place oppressive. The people within are sluggish, sifting through the clothing as if their muscles refuse to fire in time with their brain. When you step through the door, they all look up in time, their eyes wide with momentary hope, as if you've brought them something, but the moment passes and they return to their work. You only linger for a few minutes in this place. It doesn't take you long to realize the t-shirt shop is much like the first, and much like the second, only the cashier in this place is a woman, but a woman who could be part of a triplet birth with the two men. She tells you about the next store, as you know she will tell you about the next store, eyes unmoving from her screen, fingers typing in a series of digits you have no idea the correlation of.

You are outside and the ocean's roar is harsh in your ears. It's a hurricane. It's the splitting of wood. It's houses falling into the sea. It's the promised Armageddon of an entire continent swept under.

Instead of driving, you walk, following the sidewalk that leads down Route 28, covering your ears, trying to keep your thoughts straight beneath the noise. You pass shop upon shop, each a mirror image of the previous, just more dilapidated, more decayed. At some point, the storefronts are slick with algae and barnacles, streams of salt water sluicing through their parking lots like brackish estuaries. Horseshoe crabs and eel wade in the tidal pools that are their handicapped spots. Osprey nest on their roofs, leaving twined circlets of oak and pine like crowns upon their heads. Through the black mold-crusted windows, you see the others, eternally bent to their task, trying to prove their existence through a singular purchase, trying to make this moment in time matter as the ocean continues to call to them, to ask of their desires, to ask why they truly came here in the first place.

You didn't know that's what the ocean was asking, but the question is now clear, it's so loud you can't miss it, and you don't know if you have a good answer. Because everyone has been here? Because there are few other ways to prove you're actually living? Because just off the beach, staring out at the endless blue, sea and sky become indistinguishable from one another, the world inverting or going flat or consuming itself in an infinite loop that you told yourself you needed to witness. But now the ocean is screaming at you and you have no desire to see it, or be near it, or prove that you drove all this way for a stupid t-shirt and a shared experience.

Inside the nearest shop, a guttural cry goes up, bodies crashing against bodies. Through the window, you see a single arm rise out of a mass of writhing limbs, holding a maroon t-shirt aloft, before it is swept under by the rest of the things that had once been humans.

You know the size of the shirt.

There's no question in your mind.

The sea wants you to see it, to know it waits for you within.

You scream until your voice becomes hoarse. You run back to your car, passing the waterlogged storefronts, the ocean's call lessening, a shriek diminishing to a murmur then to a whispered grumble.

As you unlock the door, the female cashier steps out of the shop and waves a lazy hand in your direction. You pause.

"Today. Later today. A shipment will arrive. All sizes. All styles. All colors. You just have to wait. You just have to join us for..."

But before she can finish, you are turning the keys in the ignition. The engine's rumble replaces the sea's subtle plea.

Some trips are not worth remembering.

Footnotes to the Travel Guide

by Nicole M. Wolverton

Location: To access Pinel Island from the Saint-Martin mainland, drive through the sleepy area known as Cul-de-Sac ("cul-de-sac" translates from French to "bottom of the bag"; however, most English speakers use "cul-de-sac" to mean "dead end") on the French side of this Caribbean island and park in the lot near the dock marked "Pinel." Pay the ferryman a fee of $12 USD; you will be dropped at Pinel Island, and the fee includes a return trip. Note that the last return ferry of the day leaves Pinel Island at 4:30 PM.

Description: Formerly used to house lunatics from the mainland right around the time that slavery was abolished on Saint-Martin, Pinel Island ("pinel" is Portuguese for "crazy") has become a day-tripper's snorkeling paradise. The main beach, directly to the left of the ferry dock on the north side of the island, offers white sand and clear shallow waters that are protected from the trade winds. An ideal spot for snorkeling or sunbathing, and the two beach-side open restaurants rent chairs and umbrellas; they offer drink service as well.

To access the wilder and uninhabited south side of Pinel Island, turn right off the ferry – away from the palm and grapefruit trees that will be gently swaying in the breeze – and follow the narrow foot-path for Pinel Island Marine Trail through a lush, tropical green rush of vegetation that swallows one whole until it opens onto a short-scrubbed expanse of rocky land. Do not tarry off the trail. In addition to the north side of the island being a protected green sanctuary, there have been dozens of reports of missing persons (see conclusionary note at the end of this report).

Supernatural Manifestations: "It was just me and my boyfriend Mike," says Olive Satterwaite, who lives in Blue Ridge, Georgia. "I told him not to go, but he wanted to see the mysterious wagon everyone was telling us about. He climbed up over the little hill just before the Marine Trail descends to the beach, and that was it. I yelled his name for an hour, but the only thing that answered me back were birds. It sounded like thousands of them."

The wagon has been a legend on Pinel Island for well over a century. Satterwaite did not see the wagon on the day that Michael Blanke disappeared; however, for those who have caught a glimpse from the trail, it is described as dark green, with a curved roof stretched over with dirty white fabric. While no horse has ever been sighted, a hitch has been visible, along with a shallow grass green porch built off the entryway to the wagon.

Extensive drone footage of Pinel Island has never revealed the location of a wagon of any type, nor the bodies of the missing trail hikers. Saint-Martin authorities call claims of missing persons and sightings of the wagon "unsubstantiated."

However, local Cul-de-Sac resident Jérôme Ledee says that authorities are afraid to launch an investigation because of what they may find. "You live here long enough, you see things after dark. Lights moving around on Pinel Island, long after no one is supposed to be out there. That's why the last ferry comes back so early — you won't find anyone with sense in their head anywhere near that island when the sun goes down. Evil things live there."

When asked why the legendary wagon might be part of that evil, Ledee points to Pinel Island's dark past as a haven for the mentally ill. "No one wants to say it, but the people that were forced over there suffered, even after the cruel suffering of slavery — and many of them weren't crazy at all. Legend has it that a doctor — a white man from the States — was charged with looking after the people over there, at least for a time. He brought with him a small green wagon. You could see folks hauling it for him, up over the dunes. People say he did things on that island. To those that lived there."

Charmaine Choisy, who also lives in Cul-de-Sac, has a more sinister explanation. She says, "The wagon was no good. An ancestor escaped Pinel Island and documented it quite well. When the people who were kept on that island heard the squeak of the wheels, they'd hide — they knew that doctor was coming for them. He'd snap one of them up, and for hours all anyone would hear were screams."

Investigation: Paranormal investigators Barry Ash and Nylah Ziegler-Ash, a married couple from Philadelphia, Pennsylvania with many years of experience, were sent to Pinel Island in July 2020 with the intention of purposefully missing the final ferry back to Cul-de-Sac and exacting a thorough search of the island for any signs of the mysterious wagon or the missing hikers. A portion of the following emails, notes, recordings, and videos were received periodically over the course of that night; the remainder were recovered the next day:

[17:30 NZA *email*]

Barry and I watched the final ferry of the day leave the dock from our hiding spot in a grove of grapefruit trees and overgrown shrubs not far from the beach restaurants. We thought the restaurant employees might see us at one point; however, the second the ferry pulled away from the dock, the employees were frantic about cleaning up and closing the restaurant for the night. A bunch of them came within feet of us, but no matter what sound came from our direction, they studiously refused to even look toward the interior of the island. We even tested it out – we threw a couple of small rocks against the side of the restaurant, whispered loudly. Nothing. No reaction at all, except for the employees moving faster. By 17:15, they were all huddled together on the dock, and a speedboat picked them up, leaving me and Barry alone on Pinel Island. The sky's starting to go pink already – a pretty sunset, but that means it should be dark within the hour. It remains humid and sweaty, even with the breeze off the water.

[18:30 BA *email*]

Completed a thorough exploration of the restaurants and other out-buildings near the beach. Aside from evidence of the hasty effort to get off the island, Nylah and I found nothing out of the ordinary. Night has come, and the island feels as though it is breathing, like a hot huff of air down my neck. I know this to be nothing more than imagination, and Nylah would probably poke fun if I told her, but I admit that my heart races with each exhale. We will now take the Pinel Island Marine Trail for our first true test of the night. Nylah plans to leave the trail – however, I insist that she attach a rope to her belt. Whether or not there is, indeed, something evil on the island, I will feel better if I have some method of finding her should anything truly happen.

[19:30 BA *voice report*]

Nylah has disappeared into the scrub, and I cannot find her. I cannot raise her by cell phone nor walkie. The breathing I feel – the island breathing – grows louder, but the birds that had been chattering away are now silent. It has been forty-five minutes since Nylah left the trail, and I have not moved. The rope tied around her waist is slack, and I am afraid to continue on, lest she stumbles back to me in need of help.

[19:44 NZA *voice report*]

I found a second path! It's definitely not on any of the Pinel Island maps we looked at. I had to untie the rope that Barry insisted on, but I know he'll understand once I get back to him. I know he's probably worrying like crazy, though, and I feel a little bad about it. My cell phone service is shot, so you'll probably get all these reports in a big chunk once I get into a coverage area. Anyway, there's another path about twenty yards off the trail. What's weird, though, is I feel like I should have reached the flat part of the island already – I feel like I've been walking at least twenty minutes. The birds are putting up a real racket. Unless this path goes in circles, I should drop off into the ocean any second now. The island just isn't that big. I've stopped at a large flat rock at the base of a palm tree – at least I think it's a palm tree. I tried to get Barry on the walkie, but I think maybe the trees are causing too much interference.

[20:15 BA *voice report; ed,* Ash's voice is tense and low]

I urge you to call the Saint-Martin authorities when you receive this. Nylah is still missing, and I decided to return to the ferry dock. I must have gotten turned around, though, because I found myself back in the spot where she disappeared after ten minutes. I tried again and achieved the same result. The moon is risen but appears stuck in the sky – I do not understand, and I mostly assume it is an optical illusion. I'm trying to stay calm, but I'm worried. Very worried indeed. Instead of attempting the ferry dock, I decided to continue along the Marine Trail. I thought perhaps when I reached the south side of the shoreline that I might find other pathways through the protected area of the island, but there is nothing but the sea. I just set up emergency flares on the rocky beach on the off-chance a passing boat will notice and offer a rescue. Right now I am sitting on the beach, facing the ocean. The sound and the feel of breathing continues, and I wonder if perhaps it is the waves crashing and being sucked out again. If Nylah doesn't return soon, I may conduct the paranormal investigation without her – maybe it'll help me find her. I feel I can't wait, and perhaps I will discover a clue in the process. Maybe she's hurt.

Oh! I just heard a squeaking noise behind me, almost like metal rubbing against metal. I'll investigate and get back to you. I am hoping it's Nylah. Do let me know if you're receiving these transmissions and if you contacted the authorities.

[20:22 NZA *voice report*; *ed,* Ziegler-Ash whispers during the whole of the following transcript]

I can't believe it! I found the wagon. Barry is going to flip! I followed the hidden path I'd been on and wandered into a thicket of tall trees. The wagon is half obscured by the foliage and a tangle of thick, brown roots. [*the sound of rustling and ocean waves*] I almost walked right past it – it's so dark, and this part of the trail is so overgrown. I'm not surprised that people have only caught a glimpse of this thing, even in the daylight when it would be more visible. The air here smells strongly of salt and hibiscus, and something else. Something… dirty. I don't mean dirty as in sex-dirty, I mean like dirt. Old dirt. A light just turned on in the wagon – it's shining through the fabric top, and I swear I just saw a shadow move inside. [*clunking noises, the sound of Nylah's breath*].

Okay, I've decided to hang back in case there really is a vagrant living in the wagon. I remember you briefing us on the island, saying that it used to be home to Saint-Martin's mentally ill. I think you said it was over a hundred or two hundred years ago – so I suppose it's possible that some hermit ancestor of someone who lived here could still be living on the island. While I'm more inclined to believe just that – a human who prefers the isolation of the island – I am going to do a cursory walk-through of the site. Let Barry know I'm being careful, okay? [*a grunt and more quiet clunks*] As I said, the landscape is over-grown and hidden from view – certainly from the main Marine Trail at least, but I can't imagine it'd be easily seen from anywhere, on the island or off. The moonlight only shines through the overgrowth a little, and the wagon itself is green – almost the same green as the brush. On a dark night this whole area would be invisible. Standing next to the wagon, you can't see any lights from Saint-Martin at all. With my flashlight turned off, it's very dim – but I can still see because of the light inside the wagon. I would have expected it to be louder here – the sound of the ocean waves is somewhat muted, maybe by all the trees and bushes? I don't know, but there aren't even any birds. Every now and then I hear the faint sounds of what I assume are small animals — maybe those little lizards skittering around, or mice. The air feels very still, though, and very thick and humid. Like I said, it smells like flowers and the smell of the ocean is very strong, too. I think what I meant when I said that it smells dirty is that it smells earthy, if that makes sense.

Okay, I'm going to take some baseline images. Hold on, I'm going to switch off my recorder and move to video.

[20:51 NZA *video report*]

This is Nylah Ziegler-Ash on Pinel Island at the site of the hidden wagon on July 8, 2020 at 8:51 PM. Going quiet now. [*ed.*, video footage indicates that Ziegler-Ash crept around the scene in silence; her footsteps are audible but very quiet, and the sound of waves is similar to a dim hiss in the background. The camera does not pick up a great deal, other than thick underbrush and several trees. While

Ziegler-Ash refers to the wagon being present, it does not appear in this section of footage at all. At 21:01 the footage indicates that Ziegler-Ash found a spot in which to settle in and observe her surroundings, as the camera becomes stationary. At 21:17, the camera jolts and the image swings wildly.] A curtain across the back of the wagon just swung aside, and light from inside is giving me slightly better visibility. What looks like a human ribcage is resting on the tiny porch. [*loudly*] Hello? My name is Nylah Ziegler-Ash. I'm sorry to disturb you — I'm conducting an investigation of Pinel Island... I'm terribly sorry, sir. I didn't realize anyone was living on the island. Do you mind if I ask you a few questions?... [*ed.*, footage does not pick up the sound of a second voice, nor an image of to whom Ziegler-Ash is speaking] No, I'm not here alone — my husband is on the Marine Trail, probably waiting for me on the beach... have you lived here long?... oh, yes, I'd love to come in for a cup of tea. [*ed.*, footage indicates that Ziegler-Ash walks into a shadowed space, and her footsteps can be heard on what sound like wooden stairs. A few seconds later, hinges squeak, and bright light floods the camera. The view is of a dented wood-planked floor with dark stains — there is speculation that perhaps Ziegler-Ash did not want the subject to know they were being filmed] Thank you, Mr.... oh, Dr. Holmes. Thank you — this is so nice of you. Your little house is so hidden — you must have lived here a very long time... wow, that *is* a long time... how have you managed to evade detection? There are rumors about the island, but... and you live here alone? Oh... you know, maybe I should go — you seem busy. That's quite a collection of tools you have. I don't want to keep you from — uh, no, I wasn't aware. That's — I'll pass, thank you. It's not something I'd like to see. Did you... is there something in this tea? I feel [*Ziegler-Ash's shoes come into view — brown hiking boots with blue laces — and she appears to be staggering. Seconds later, she falls to her knees, then collapses to the floor. The camera points at her chin, picking up Ziegler-Ash's mouth.*] Let me... no... I... please let... [*A force pulls Ziegler-Ash quickly away from the camera, and her body is flung backward and up at an angle. She lands heavily on the floor seconds later with a high-pitched groan. The camera struggles to focus on a small white*

object that bounces toward it until finally the focus crys-
tallizes on a single molar. Ziegler-Ash's breathing is wet –
and she is yanked backward again and lands off camera
with a hard thud. What looks like blood splashes across
the floor. Ziegler-Ash screams for the next twenty min-
utes, then falls silent. The lights go out, and the screen is
dark once more. Several sounds are picked up in the next
33 minutes, but nothing definitive. We assume the battery
power failed at 22:00, as there is nothing more recorded
on the camera beyond that point.[1]]

[22:07 BA *voice report; ed.*, Ash's voice is ragged, his
words rushed – as if he is running]

It won't stop. It's been hours – it follows, and a
woman... been hearing screams, horrible screams. It
sounds like my Nylah, but I can't... whenever I turn
toward it, it gets in front of me and seems to come

---

1 Audio recordings from Ziegler-Ash's phone and camera were
analyzed for electronic voice phenomenon (EVP). Several anomalies
were picked up, particularly when Ziegler-Ash was inside the wagon.
At 21:19, a low voice is heard to growl, "come in," and at 20:24 we
hear several voices laughing, which continues for well over a fifteen
minute period. Outside the wagon, a voice can be heard whispering
"Holmes comes," "please go," and "no" at various points.

straight for... the squeak of the wheels, whatever is... not sure if you're getting these... I'm in trouble. Have to find Nylah. Can't shake it. The island... the whole island... breathing, breathing, like I'm in the lungs of some awful thing. God, help me!

[22:32 BA *voice report*; *ed.*, the VM opens with Ash screeching. When he speaks, his voice is high-pitched and panicked.]

Oh, god. Oh god! I found a body, and so help me I think it's Nylah. It's her pack on the ground. The body is – oh my god. [*Ash screams and gibbers.*] Oh god, Nylah, hang on, baby. You have to send help right now – she's alive. Nylah, sweetie, what... is that... is that the wagon? [*Ash screams again, and the phone goes dead.*]

Conclusion: Barry Ash was discovered at approximately 08:00 the following morning by employees of the restaurants on Pinel Island. He was found, lying face-down, at the entrance to the Marine Trail. His equipment, as well as Nylah Ziegler-Ash's bag and equipment, were found with him. Ash suffered several injuries too gruesome to describe. Those that found him report that he could do nothing but whimper, although he did scream the words "wagon" and "Holmes," as well as Nylah's name, until he succumbed to his injuries at approximately 08:57. Nylah Ziegler-Ash's body has never been recovered. Since her disappearance, at least two other hikers have gone missing. We cannot rule out a murderous person living in a wagon on Pinel Island; however, given the EVP work done inside and outside the alleged wagon, as well as the disturbing footage from inside the wagon, we feel comfortable labeling the island haunted, and dangerously so. Do not risk staying on Pinel Island after the last ferry leaves for the day — and do not, under any circumstances, go in search of the wagon (which we assume to be the source of the haunting) at any time of day.

St. Cecilia's Catacomb Is or Isn't Real, but Hear Me Out!

by DeBussy O'Slamahain

There is something the Catholic Church isn't telling you. Well, there are many things they aren't telling you, but there's one thing in particular that warrants your attention. Tell me, you have heard of the catacombs in Italy and France, right? The history of them is quite fascinating and a touching devotion to the lives lost with time, and some of them are saints. But let me tell you about a catacomb I visited once that left me a different person to this day.

So, it was in the countryside of Italy that this catacomb resided. My actual destination was to my grandma's childhood villa. It wasn't too far from my hostel but gran-gran never mentioned living so close to a freaking catacomb. Despite the care and attention paid to the building and the surrounding area, there was a dilapidated air about the place.

DeBussy O'Slamahain

Like it was screaming "DO NOT COME, DO NOT ENTER." Despite the Kamala Harris impersonation, I was taken in with the quaint aesthetic. A real cottage core meets a beautiful goth farmer looking to remake rococo tombs from memory and scratch.

There was an inch of water pooling about in the fountains by the entrance, and the only guests there besides myself were the occasional brave woodland creatures, demanding penance for encroaching on their homeland. I took a star off my Yelp review because the squirrel bit my finger when I offered it a piece of my panini.

Going inside, the elderly priest jolted back to life and greeted me with a scratchy voice. You could mistake him for one of his brothers on the wall, but he had much more skin and dressed more modern. He almost dropped the euros I offered him and began to ramble about saints. I mean, it was cute at first. He spoke of those old bones as if he wined and dined them when they were alive (and hopefully with flesh and such). Even with the cute little ticket in hand and the glazed over gazes of the dead around us, Father Greeter reminisced on.

After he stopped, from what seemed like hours, I got to walk about the catacomb. The deeper I went in, the more something in my stomach turned. Longing and wistful. Mummified faces smiled back at me and I began to feel like I would be one with them one day. I got to a dead end with skulls and various bones used as décor to surround the body of a small girl. Her white dress was stained with red where she held something; I couldn't tell what it was.

Our Miracle was engraved above her head. And the closer I looked to the mummified jelly in the sea of red, the pile of my soul began to struggle. A thousand eyes were upon me, and before I could turn to face the source, the mummified girl gripped onto me.

"You weren't supposed to stop here," a raspy voice hissed, and just like that, my vision turned to black.

How I got back to my hostel I couldn't tell you. My fellow hostel mates said I just came home and silently went to my room. I tried telling them about the catacomb and showed them the ticket but they just laughed at me. My ticket was a gas station receipt for bread and water in the amount I paid to visit the saints.

But I'm telling you it's real, and you shouldn't visit St. Cecilia's catacomb. She doesn't want you there, and it's better off you don't piss her off.

The Ghost of Yareuva IV

by Dewi Hargreaves

People don't think about refuelling stations very much.

You can't blame them. They have places to be. Nobody travels across space to see a glorified gas depot, after all. Refuelling stations are stopping points, waymarks along the journey, inconveniences that must be stomached while we buy an expensive sandwich and stretch our legs. We're physically there — but mentally we've already left, so the station exists in a half-reality, a spirit on interstellar winds.

How do you think the station feels about that?

***

The last time I passed through Sector 042, I was on a freight mission. I stopped at the refuelling station of Yareuva IV — my engine light had been blinking for several systems, and my patience with it had finally run out.

I hung around the depot while they brought out the huge fuel pipes, which always reminded me of hydra heads, and attached them to my freighter's fuselage. An officer asked me the usual questions — contraband? No. Trading license? Yes. Where you going? Where you from? Do you know where the toilets are?

It was only supposed to take a moment, but I knew bad news was coming by the look on the engineer's face. They'd found a fault in my jump drive — a sparkplug had been chewed through by a rat or something. Apparently I was lucky I wasn't thrown out of jumpspace mid-flight, left to drift for the next one thousand years in the black space between solar systems. But then, people always told me I was lucky.

"It'll take a few hours," the engineer said in his gruff, gravelly voice. "Make yourself comfortable."

I groaned. "Do you at least know where the toilets are?"

I found things to do. I lingered in an overpriced and especially grotty branch of Spacefarer's Coffee Co., I sipped a bitter cup of coffee — no sugar, never sugar — and I nibbled a lukewarm chicken sandwich purchased from a hot bench manned by an android whose rat-brown paint was starting to flake off. I searched for the toilets and eventually found them, after following far too many blue signs down far too many corridors. I waited. I thought about the shipping lanes ahead, the level of traffic, the planet I was heading towards and how long it might take me to get there, and how far away home was. I sweated; the station's life support was bugging out and nobody could get the thermostats working, so everyone dripped and everyone stank. Interstellar turbulence rattled the station several times, sending the unexpecting stumbling, and spilling coffee down dirty jumpsuits.

"Who was Yareuva?" I asked a bored-looking barista, who shrugged and gave me one of those looks — the look that tells you nobody has ever asked or thought of that question before, and you are exceedingly weird for being the first, and you should never think or ask it again.

"I don't know," she said. Her makeup was pristine, and I'd never seen a tighter-bound ponytail. "A pioneer or something. Don't you have places to be?"

That's the thing about these stations: even the folks who work there, who spend hours there each day, are somewhere else. They're slapping spacefarer-brand stickers on polyburgers and astro coffee, but they're already thinking of what they'll do when they clock out. This place doesn't exist to them – it's where they earn money. There is no deeper meaning. Nobody cares.

With no choice but to wait until my ship was repaired, I did what anyone would. I found a seat on the main promenade, I sat, and I people-watched.

There were the usual suspects, yes – commuters from the nearby planet of New Silesia on their ways to wherever. I saw long-haul freighters from further afield. There were even some from the First Systems – vast interstellar ships that had come from Earth, Mars, or Venus and were continuing on to, in some cases, the end of the galaxy. I realised this place was not so barren at all. It had many grasping hands, and they reached far; the folks who stopped here would carry half-memories of this place to more locations than they individually could visit in a lifetime.

There were recurring colours in the jumpsuits
I saw: the bright vermillion and deep maroon hues
of Red Star Salvage, and the orange and white of
Resource Extraction Ltd. The two groups mostly kept
to themselves, moving in clusters like tribal packs,
though some did speak amiably to each other in the
food queues, and several even drank and laughed
together. I took it as a sign of thawing relations,
which made me hopeful. I could never have guessed
at the brutal war that followed, which claimed thousands of lives — and resulted, ultimately, in Yareuva
IV's destruction.

I hung around until the end of the day, when
the station's internal clock — timed to the nearest
inhabited planet — told us it was night. The light
dulled, becoming a liminal, unpleasant glow that
reminded me of the front lobby of a big-chain hotel.
The janitors came out to clean through the sleeping
hours, ready for tomorrow.

The gruff engineer found me. He had bad news.
"We need an extra part. Guy's on his way, but won't
arrive till tomorrow. Make yourself comfortable."

"You said that already."

"Did I?" he couldn't have looked less bothered. "I lose track. So many of you, you know."

I followed purple signs to the hostel, which was full of naval academy youths on their gap years, sweating and crawling into bed with each other. I decided I'd rather sleep on a bench on the promenade, outside the coffee shop.

A janitor swept passed me with his mechanical mop. His back was stooped and his face was so wrinkled I could hardly find his eyes. Three wisps of hair stood in the centre of his cranium and white tufts clutched his ears like missed patches of grass.

"No room at the inn?" he asked. His voice was warm.

"It's quieter out here."

"It is, isn't it?" he glanced around and took a big breath, giving a contented sigh. "This is my favourite time. Everything slows down. You can feel the station beneath you. So many just hurry through, never looking around."

I sat up and peered a little closer at him. "How long have you worked here?"

He waved dismissively. "Oh, a while. Pretty much since the start. Everything ran much better then. The spacelord doesn't spend as much as he should on maintenance — just wants to collect his business rents."

"Who was Yareuva?"

The man's eyes lit up. "Yareuva! A modest woman, passionate about comfortable interstellar travel. As modest as she was boring and unremarkable, but she would be especially happy to know there are still people asking after her, all these years later."

"Passionate about comfortable interstellar travel," I repeated with a chuckle. "Not a subject you hear much about."

"It's one of those invisible services, isn't it? Nobody thinks about Yareuva IV, but I guarantee they'd notice if it was gone. It's like air or water. You don't think much about it till you really need it."

"Do you miss Yareuva?"

"No, no." His eyes sparkled. "Yareuva still lives. Look around you. We are cells in an organism, moving here and there, doing our things to keep this station running. It's a consciousness that changes every day, assembled from the stories and memories of everyone who stops here. There is nothing to miss, because she is not gone."

The janitor moved on, humming as he mopped. The strange encounter sank into me, settled in my thoughts.

Been here since the start, he'd said.

"Wait. How old would that make you?"

I looked around, but the janitor was nowhere to be seen.

His words had a profound effect on me. I saw the station differently. I saw it for the fulcrum it was — invisible, yes, but incredibly important. And overlooked. I mused on the idea of cataloguing the stations I passed through — of writing about their quirks and histories, of making a book about them, something that would give them a presence, make people appreciate them.

But then I moved on. And everyone moved on. And I forgot about it. Because, really, I'd only spent a day there, and there was much else to think about, and many other places to spend much more time.

And the phantom of Yareuva continued to linger on the outskirts of the system, its single amber guide-light blinking like a buoy on a stormy ocean. A friend that tells you *yes, you're in the right place, keep going*, but whom you never thank, and never really think about, until they, too, are gone one day.

Translocation 101

by Harley Showers

A large silver mirror stands on the edge of a desk at the end of the hall. Runic carvings etched in its frame sequentially glow as the reflective surface fades to black. Suddenly, a projection of ethereal purple light exudes out from the object and outlines images. Vast tree trunks with gnarled branches twisting around one another line the background as vines heave below their immensity. The purple shifts into a murky green portrait as a figure with pale blue robes and tarnished spectacles steps into the frame.

"Ah hello and welcome to Translocation 101. I am Professor Verloren Inakronym and today we will be exploring the dangers of translocation and the importance of ecology," the figure waves their hand.

"With me today is my research assistant, Wilburn, who will be recording our excursion via the Crown of Oculary Redistribuation. Isn't that right, Wilburn?" The image shifts up and down.

"Wilburn, haven't I told you nodding is indistinct and unassertive?" Inakronym raises an eyebrow at the frame.

A shrill voice responds: "Ah, well. Yes, sir. But I was thinking I wouldn't speak very much during this endeavor, sir. So it will more immerse the students who watch, which is to say it will seem to them they are actually following you, sir."

Inakronym tugs at the end of his goatee while staring at the forest floor.

Wilburn pipes in again before the professor can speak. "Also, sir... we are in Knoteye so perhaps it's best only one of us does the talking?"

The professor peers up with a sharp smile towards his assistant. "I suppose such a notion has merit. Fascinating concept, Wilburn. Of course, do speak up if you experience any bodily harm."

A distinctive gulping noise can be heard out of frame as Wilburn chokes out, "Y-yes, sir."

"Very astute on your second point as well." Verloren folds his hands behind his back and stiffens his shoulders. "Today I have translocated us to the middle of Knoteye forest. Quite possibly the most dangerous place on the Calcerian continent. You see, when translocating it is very important to be prepared for such occasions when magic acts finicky as it is often wont to do."

Verloren closes his eyes and pauses briefly. "Ahem, in simple terms we are here to show you how hostile some places may be so you are not inclined to transport yourselves on any free-spirited whim."

As Inakronym steps towards Wilburn he is thrown ass over tea kettle and lifted in the air by a vine clinging to his legs. Wilburn lets out a small shriek and shifts his focus upwards, revealing the professor's under-briefs and a pair of cozy slippers embroidered with meticulously made manticores.

"Ahah, you see dear students, this was the exact type of thing I was warning of. Now, Wilburn, I believe the safest course of action is for you to cut me down and for us to run away before this vegetation decides to digest me." Verloren speaks swaying from side to side, his ponytail hanging in the mud as the image in the mirror shifts up and down once more.

A flurry of stalky silhouettes race by as the sound of exasperated breaths echoes from the mirror. The shapes steady into grays and browns as Wilburn comes to a stop. The angle sharply changes from the dense trees to the detritus-soiled earth.

"Eh... heh. Well done, Wilburn!" Inakronym says from off to the side. "Who knew carnivorous flora could uproot itself? Did you get that on the crown?"

The image shifts from side to side and moves to the master wizard. His robes are torn from briars, and puffy red rings wrap around his left ankle. Though the manticore slippers are pristine.

"Well, damn!" Verloren says while tugging mud from his ponytail. "Running for one's life does make it difficult to catch such visuals. Perhaps a more passive approach is required."

Nodding, Wilburn looks upward, the canopy is a vast black expanse with flecks of deep green.

"It's gotten dark quite quickly, we were only running a short while."

Wilburn sighs deeply and glances at the professor meticulously plucking thorns from his robes while nestling on the ground. In the far scattered woods behind him a faint halo of light bounces along repetitively. A short stalky hand enters the frame and points to the emanation.

"Wretched things!" Verloren says still prying thorns until noticing Wilburn's indication. "Oh, well, that could be interesting. A luminescent insect or perhaps a will o' wisp. Come, Wilburn, best approach with caution." Inackronym stands with a giddy trepidation and marches off towards the source of illumination.

Wilburn whispers under his breath, "Ora help us." The mirror's view moves upward and follows after the disheveled wizard.

The path towards the ever-moving light is met with overgrown roots and slick hillocks of mud. Professor Inakronym leaps into the air and glides over many of the obstacles while Wilburn struggles to climb over them. After trekking for hours, the illumination steadies its movement. The wizard wildly stomps off towards the source while Wilburn carefully steps over forest debris and muck.

The mirror's view shows Inakronym standing behind the trunk of a large elm tree in the dim light. A distant snapping sound rings out from behind

Wilburn who stops dead. The professor quickly tucks behind the tree and peers at his assistant with a finger raised to his lips.

Wilburn turns from side to side in search of the noise; nothing but the foliage of Knoteye lingers around him. The mirror pans to his muddy boots as he lifts them slowly and plants them cautiously with each step towards Inakronym who continues his skulking. Reaching the elm, Wilburn's hands clutch its bark as he peers at the light they followed.

A series of ravaged bedrolls lay strewn across the ground. Beside them a man with sun-scarred skin hunches over a pile of gray dust. Across from the man, sitting on a willow root, is a fellow who stands no higher than Verloren's knee. He tinkers with something in his hands. Behind both figures stands a woman with silken auburn hair and ornate garments. In her hand a slender stick emits a dull halo of light at its end.

"Professor, we should introduce ourselves," Wilburn says faintly, turning towards his employer.

Inakronym rears his head at his companion with burning eyes and mouths the word no.

Glancing back at the recently discovered group, a bright orange flame spreads light from a lantern held by the gnomish man, who promptly sets it on one of the blood-soaked bedrolls. The taller man holds up three fingers towards the woman who nods in response. The trio then turn deeper towards the forest beyond.

"Professor," Wilburn huffs a whisper.

"They could be murderers," Inakronym hisses.

As the gnome reaches for the handle of the lantern, the flame inside burns a bright red.

"They don't look like murderers, sir," Wilburn says shifting his view between the camp and his compatriot.

"Murderers have a look, do they?"

"That's not—"

An insidious screech falls across the forest and the sound that follows can only be described as a large pale of water being hurled against a boulder from a long distance. The mirror's view fixates on the campsite and the trio turns to see an amorphous red mass before them.

A timid "eep" comes from Verloren, but the mirror remains on the campsite.

The sun-scarred man heaves an axe from his side into his hands and rushes towards the crimson blob.

"No!" the auburn-haired woman screams.

The mass moves like water and takes shape into a beast with legs and arms that end in pointed claws. The man, still rushing forward, stops as he is split open down the middle by one of the creature's lashing appendages and falls into a heap of blood and gore.

"Professor, do something!" Wilburn now yells.

The gnome continuously paces backwards from the horror of his fallen comrade while the woman steps forward shouting at the bloody beast.

"Back you foul creature! By Val' adria's name go back from whence you came!" A giant golden beam of light erupts from the tip of her wand and streaks towards the creature. Its claw reaches up and clasps the incoming energy. A tangle of red liquid bubbles up the golden beam towards the sorceress.

"Damnit Inakronym help them!" Wilburn faces the wizard.

Verloren's gaze lingers wide-eyed at the carnage and is only stirred by his assistant's plea. He nods, flicks his wrist, and begins reciting arcane jargon.

Turning back, the red liquid continues stretching across the beam like a pulsating vein. The creature screeches from some unseen orifice repeatedly until it turns into a distorted inhuman laughter. The golden light fades as the liquid lunges forward past the sorceress's wand and clings to the skin of her hand. Then red mist bursts from her form as every ounce of blood in her body is pulled through her pores and ricochets back to the creature which doubles in size.

Wilburn looks back to Inakronym. Still muttering an absurd incantation, the professor outstretches his arm and extends his index finger and pinky into a fork. A spark surges between the two fingers as he twists his forearm upward and finishes his eldritch ramblings. Lightning crackles out of his hand, past the surrounding trees and into the liquid mass. The creature shrieks and ungulates from the electrical pulses rippling across its form.

"Now, we run again!' Inakronym shouts as Wilburn sees him rushing away from the creature.

Wilburn passes the great elm tree and scans the ground. "Ah... little guy if you're still here we got to go!"

"Who you calling little?" The head of the gnome pops out from under an arched tree root.

A sloshing roar echoes from behind them. Wilburn turns to see the flailing liquid mass has shaped itself the head of a grand dragon.

"Don't have to tell me twice," the gnome says speeding along with the lantern in hand.

Wilburn quickly follows behind. Still hearing the shock-stunted cries of the abomination. He catches up to the gnome who breathes heavier with each step. In the distance the blue robes of Professor Inakronym guide their direction.

"You should drop the lantern, it's less weight," Wilburn says, his breath faltering between the words.

"No way. Finders, keepers," the gnome shouts, his hand clenching the handle of the object. "Besides, it's our only light."

"Hopefully we won't need it much longer," Wilburn says as ahead of them Inakronym runs through wisps of ground-clinging fog.

"Sure," the gnome replies. "It's Sidwitt by the way, my friends cal– called me Sid."

"Wilburn. What were you doing here?"

"Invest – teh – gate – ing disa – pearances," Sid's voice heaves as the fog grows thicker around them. "You?"

"Eh... research," Wilburn says as his rapid inhalations are picked up by the crown.

The light in the mirror dims slightly as the lantern shifts from red back to a dull orange. No sounds but that of the two men emit from the mirror. They both pause, listening to the lingering quiet.

"Professor, are you here?" Wilburn says, calling into the fog.

A heavy splash rings from a few feet away. Pacing forward, the two search. Mist fills the mirror for several minutes before a faint gasp escapes Wilburn followed by several thuds and another splash.

Boggy water courses over the vision in the mirror. Then more mist and the light of the lantern from above.

"You alright, kid?" Sid whispers.

"Mildly," Wilburn calls back, his hands pressing into the muddy shore. Next to him, upon his exit, sits Inakronym, soaked and leering downward. At the same time, Sid is heard sliding down the muddy hill far more gracefully.

"Professor, you need to translocate us back to Bulwart's or anywhere really," Wilburn says, touching the wizard's shoulder.

"Oh, Wilburn, it's dreadful, my slippers are ruined," Inakronym mutters.

Wilburn focuses on the once cozy slippers now stained with mud and absent the embroidered manticores except for vague faces. Sid passes by and looks out at the water, lantern held high.

"We'll clean your slippers when we get back." Wilburn says, trying to peer at the old man's face.

"I can't clean them," the professor stutters.

"I didn't know there was a swamp in Knoteye," Sid says. "There is water everywhere."

Wilburn glances around upon Sid's words, revealing mounds of dirt surrounded by water and each adorned with piles of rocks.

"We'll get you new ones then." Wilburn finally responds to the wizard.

"I can't clean them. I can't. No energy left," Inackronym says.

"What? Professor we need to leave immediately before that thing comes back," Wilburn pleads.

"I used it all. And it just stood there stunned. No burns or exploding into a mess of ash," Inackronym rambles as Wilburn grabs the collar of his robes.

The surrounding light shifts to a dull green.

"How far from the forest edge are we, Verloren?" Wilburn shouts.

"There are an awful lot of stones for a bog," Sid's voice calls from out of view. "I think these might be ca—"

"There's no way of knowing. The only hope is rest. But we won't make it through the night," Inackronym says in a panic.

"He's... right..."

Sid's meager voice echoes outward through the forest, but another timber and cadence overlaps with his. Wilburn glances upward, seeing Sid floating in the air just under the mist. His head twisted backward, chin resting on his patterned vest, and eyes glass white. Wilburn goes to stand but is lashed back down. To either side, vines tangle his wrists and feet.

"Poor meager mortals came to play in the woods. Knowing of the danger. Yet, still venturing forth. Only to die here in Knoteye." Each syllable exits Sid's mouth as if the upper jaw was pulled by a string. "Someone must have a lot to prove." The corpse's head jostles toward the professor. "Silly old wizard never could do anything right, just always runs from his problems like the frightened coward he is." Sid's backwards arms clasp onto Inackronym's tattered robes.

"No... no, please no." Verloren chokes out the words.

"We're going to play with you." The corpse's face presses against Inackronym's. "See what sounds you make, maybe bring your bloody friend back." The corpse lifts the wizard and throws him. Several crashes and snaps resonate in the direction then a loud thud.

Wilburn grunts uncontrollably as the corpse floats above him, the green light reflecting off its paling face.

"Oh, you were just dragged here," the corpse says in a tone of sympathy. "You wanted to leave the moment you came. Don't worry, we'll make this quick." The floating ghoul flicks its wrist and a whelp of pain from Wilburn follows. Looking down, he sees a blood covered tree root jutting from his chest. Peering back up, he hears the corpse again.

"That'll do. Oh, and you won't be needing this anymore." The corpse reaches its hand down and, with a single finger, presses against the image in the mirror, causing cracks in the vision and the color to fade. "I hope you all enjoyed the show," the stacked voices of the corpse laugh before flying away.

The canopy of Knoteye continues losing color until a dark gray floods the mirror. A series of cackles, screams, and roars can be heard from far off until the vision goes black and the cracks dissipate.

A man in simple green robes and a chinstrap beard steps out from behind the desk while tapping the mirror's frame. The carved runes dim and the reflective surface returns to the silver mirror.

"Class, that was your first lesson in Translocation 101," the man says. "Now, I may just be an adjunct professor, but I recommend dropping this course and taking Transmutation. That's where the money is."

Waiting Room

by Steve Novak

As soon as I stepped inside, I saw her. The flash of movement as she jumped up out of her chair. At first, I thought nothing of it, but half a moment later my blood started pumping as she rushed straight at me. Not knowing her intentions, I quickly backpedaled. I was pretty sure she wasn't coming for me — although you can never be sure in a situation like that — but just wanted out. So I held the door open for her. Good thing, because she didn't look like she was about to slow down. I think she would have gone right through the glass if I hadn't. Three steps across the sidewalk she pulled up. She looked around, then shouted, "Shit!" She turned and walked back inside, looking me up and down as she passed.

I followed her. She went to the counter and pulled a number.

"One-Three-Five-Six!" she said loudly.

"One-Three-Five-Five!" someone answered, and raised their hand.

The woman looked at them and nodded, then went back to her table. It was then that I noticed it. The place was different. It had changed since I was there, here, I mean there... Oh, whatever!... the day before yesterday. Yesterday, my time, or what should be my time. Gah! It still confuses me. Let me explain.

The café I stepped into was not the one I walked into. No, that's not helping. The café I entered was not the one I should have been in. It was in the same place, but it was not in the same time. You see, I passed through a time portal when I went through the door. And I wasn't the only one. But I didn't know that at the time.

It wasn't until after the woman sat down that I saw the extent of the changes. I should have noticed when she pulled the ticket. That wasn't there the last time I was. Also, I didn't recognize the woman behind the counter. Not that that was at all odd, new baristas showed up regularly, but they didn't dress like that. And the décor. Retro, is how I'd describe it.

Thinking about it, that's how I'd describe the woman behind the counter's outfit, too.

Even with the excitement of almost being run over and the change of décor, I didn't think anything was wrong. Just different. These corporate coffee shops redo things periodically, and they can make the changes practically overnight, so it wasn't a big deal. A person having some sort of moment wasn't that abnormal either. Maybe she'd forgotten something, or saw someone outside and was trying to reach them. Nothing to be concerned about, at any rate.

I had gone in for a coffee, so I went to the counter. I pulled a number because I'd seen the running woman do it, then stepped back, waiting for my number to be called. It seemed strange, but I'd been in little bakeries that still used them. The woman behind the counter looked at me.

"What'll you have?"

I looked down at my number.

"I think somebody's ahead of me."

"Oh, the numbers aren't for ordering, they're for the door."

"Huh?"

"You need to call out your number. Whoever has the number in front of yours will call out theirs and raise their hand, so you know who you go after. We had to make things more orderly, it was getting a little out of control."

"Huh?"

"Go ahead, call it out."

She waved her hand in a sign that showed me I should do it.

"One-Three-Five-Seven," I said, not very loud.

"One-Three-Five-Six!" running woman blurted out and looked at me.

I nodded.

"So what'll it be?"

I turned back around.

"Medium coffee," I said.

"Only got one size, son," she said. "You'll learn."

I took my coffee, in an actual mug, a plain, dull white, rather small mug, and found a table. I pulled out my laptop; I had work to do. No wifi. It must be down again. That's okay, I could work without it. And safe from doom scrolling. But my attention did wander. Several people came in, through the same door I had, and although no one jumped up and rushed at them, I looked up every time it opened. It wasn't the people themselves coming in that distracted me, though I have to admit a few of the young people did catch my eye, it was how they were dressed. I should say, how they looked. I mean their outfits and their hair styles. Like the woman behind the counter, the only way I can describe it is retro. Even the guys. They looked like they were extras in old TV shows, like Mayberry or that Beaver kid.

What I really should have noticed, and seen sooner, was the scene outside when the door opened. What I would normally see was a shopping center across the street, with a busy parking lot. Instead, there were a couple of old-style houses and an open field. It was so out of place it took my brain a long time to register it. When it finally did, I had to get up and go take a look.

If things were weird inside the café, they were a whole lot weirder outside. There were more houses, not a one modern looking, and all with big yards. The road was paved, but looked more gravelly than it should. And it was mostly empty, except for one or two cars parked on it. Vintage cars, I should add. There were more trees and shrubs than should have been there, and there were barns. Barns on farms. What the hell?

I wondered if I'd hit my head somehow. Had the woman who ran at me knocked me down and caused me to hit my head on the cement? Was I hallucinating? I went back inside, but this time, when I opened the door, I kept to the side and peeked around it before stepping in. Several people looked up at me with anticipation, but no one jumped out of their seats. It seemed they recognized me and were slightly disappointed. That didn't make me feel better.

I sat back down at my computer, but I couldn't work. I was too busy being confused. I got another cup of coffee. I realized I hadn't paid for the first one.

"What kind of money you got?" the waitress asked. I'm calling her a waitress because that's what she was, as you'll see.

"Do you take ApplePay?"

She smiled.

"What's your name, hun?"

"Tracy."

She pulled out a large hardcover ledger book and opened it to a blank page. At the top she wrote my name. On the first line she wrote 'Coffee' in cursive, and then two hash marks.

"Cash money, if you have the right kind, which I'm sure you don't, so I'll keep you in my ledger and you pay me when you can."

"Huh?"

She refilled my mug.

"You'll learn."

***

There were theories. Some sounded plausible, others... not so much. But no one really knew. Those that eventually got out never returned, so we got no intel from them.

The name of the café was The Waiting Room. That wasn't what it was called originally. It was changed as kind of a joke, but it was fitting, because that's what it had become, and what it was when I showed up.

The first person known to come through the portal was Bob. Bob caused quite a kerfuffle. It would have been much worse if one of us others were the first. Because Bob only came from three days in the future. I stepped back seventy years.

But poor Bob. He probably could have made out pretty well, but things didn't quite go as well as they could have.

"Going to take your mare to the auction," Francis asked him.

"What are you on about? I took her yesterday."

"Auction's the day after tomorrow. What are you going on about?"

"Yesterday. You been at the bottle, or what?"

"Today's Tuesday, auction's Thursday, same as it's been all my life. Sarah been putting something in your peas?"

"Today's Friday. Sold the mare yesterday. Got the cash right here."

Bob pulled a wad of bills out of his pocket and waved it under Francis's nose.

"Now, I'm going up to the counter and I'm going to spend some of this here money on a slice of pie and a glass of lemonade. You should go see the doc."

Well, Bob had to relive three days, and if he'd been smart, he could have profited from it. Bob was not smart. He also got into the same argument with his wife on Wednesday night that he'd had the first time. He lost both times. Poor Bob.

Nobody knows how many people have come through, or how many made it back, though we know some have. Some never will, most by choice. And then there's Coma Guy. He's a sad case. Came through the portal, sort of freaked out, turned around, and tripped. Fell face first into the sidewalk and has been in a coma ever since. The ones who left the Waiting Room without going back through the portal are, we assume, living their lives out there. Are they changing history? Throwing the timeline out of whack? We don't know. If they are, we can't see it here. Maybe when we get back. I say when, not if, though my hope fades by the day.

I've been here eight months now, and I've got things pretty well figured out, at least in regard to the Waiting Room. Here's what I know. The portal appears to be completely random. At least no one here had been able to determine any discernable pattern. Suddenly, at any time, it could open and in would walk someone from another time period. They could come from the past or future, but since the portal is, or seems to be, in the exact same location as the door to the café, the vast majority of those here are from the future. Because this place has been a café since it was built in nineteen forty-eight, the odds of someone from the past coming through are low. Apparently, it remains a café for at least another fifty or so years after my time. Could be longer, maybe somebody else will come through from further on.

So what do we do here in the Waiting Room? Mostly, we wait. We drink a lot of coffee, occasionally eat pie — it is wonderful pie, I've got to say — and sometimes a sandwich. Our phones are useless, so most people, after the initial bout of photo taking right after they arrive, don't even bother with them anymore. I use my laptop to write. None of the time-locals, as we call them, bat an eye at it anymore. Some people go out and do odd jobs to earn some money, but most sit here and wait. The place closes at eight o'clock and we all get kicked out. We've rented a house a couple of blocks away that we all share. Since it's mostly just for sleeping, it works out pretty well. Beds, cots, and padding pretty much fill up the place. We don't need anything else. In the morning we all flock down to the café, in the evening we all plod home. Those that work throw their earnings in a pot to pay for everything, the house and the café tabs. We don't talk about our home time period or our lives there. We think it might jinx things, or we just don't want to know. It's become taboo. We just don't.

The first time I saw someone make it back through the portal was a bit of a shock. It was Tanya. The door opened, we saw it was a traveler (we decided that was a better term than victim), and it was Tanya's turn. She leapt up and sprinted towards the door. Practically ran the fellow over who was coming in, and Poof! she was gone. Simply disappeared. But here's the thing: we have no idea where she went. Did she go back to her original time, the time the guy who just came in came from, or somewhen else? We have no way of knowing. We want to believe we go back to our own original time, but as with everything related to the portal, all we have are theories and ideas, some possible and some not.

More often than not, what happens, though, is what happened when I came through. The person whose turn it is races to the door, but when they get there the portal's already closed. That sucks. It happened to me. You get all your hopes up, and Wham! you're shut down. And you have to go to the back of the line.

That's where the numbers come in. From what I've been told, it used to be chaos. When someone who was obviously from the future came through the door, there was a mad rush. It got a bit ugly at times. Finally, someone came up with the idea of the numbers, and everyone agreed to it. For new people, like me, that was just the system and we didn't question it.

It's getting a little more crowded in here, with more people coming in than getting out, even with those that have given up and gone out to live in this time. I have to admit, it's crossed my mind; it doesn't seem like too bad a time to have lived. But then I remember it wasn't all sunshine and roses back then, not for everybody. Back now. Or here. Oh, you know what I mean.

So here I sit, waiting my turn. There's about ten people in front of me now, so I figure I've got another few months until my next chance. Fingers crossed.

stranger things have happened

by Devaki Devay

Dear mummy, pappa,

You won't believe where I am if I say it outright, so I'm going to start from the beginning. And I know you'll have all kinds of criticisms – that I should've called, or stopped elsewhere, or planned better, not just this trip, but life in general. I bet your anger will sing me back to the world, and if not that, at least I'll feel a sting.

The truth is, I've never started from the beginning of anything. Rather I pick up a story from some reputable or amorphous spot in the middle, like when I told you about my girlfriend, but not the party; the feeling better, but not the therapy. Well, now you know about the therapy. It starts there.

I'll admit I was in limbo, and maybe I'll even admit
the philosophy degree was a part of it – and I know
you'll say my depression was economic, and my
stagnancy a self-constructed academic sabotage.
You'll say philosophy is the study of being stuck, and
if I'd learnt to build, I could've engineered my way
out of this, and my doctor cousin Sanjay would've
put a defibrillator to his own heart and realigned the
beats, but I think I was meant to wander around this
empty, horizontal plane, while everyone I knew lifted
upwards like colorful balloons.

So I told my therapist how I felt. I know you'll say
I should've told you – maybe. But I wanted it to be
with a stranger. Maybe I wanted to even be a little
impressive about it.

And he was impressed, you know. Very interested. I
looked him in his fishbowl eyes and told him how
I didn't think I was meant for the planet because I
couldn't see myself ending up anywhere. So he asked
me about my beginnings, to get to know me, and I
told him the story about how you, my parents, spent

a long time finding an American city for us to begin, driving like the country was a supermarket and each new apartment a fruit to pick up, investigate, and put down upon finding a bruise. I told him about the hotels, the vending machine milk warmed in the microwaves, the gas station sandwiches, the vomit in the backseat. I told him about our moving truck, the sandy roads spinning behind us, erecting into cities, and dribbling back down into stout trees.

I was so young I can only see it clearly in my dreams, where the memory is still undisturbed and waiting. My therapist told me the way to solve my issues was to take a road trip. He said it was a little unconventional, but at the time it sounded more like fun than a warning. I should've noticed... but anyway, you'll give me that lecture on your own.

I completed half of it. I was going to tell you, but I didn't know how to justify it — you'd need to know where I was going, and the truth was that I wasn't going anywhere, like usual, just following a path, and this was the middle of it. In Indiana, a memory returned to me, very specific: a hard candy packet at the gas station filled with mini bananas.

You treat me as if I've forgotten everything. I wish I could explain that my adulthood is not yours, that I've lived so much less life than you still, and if I stretch out my arm back in time, I can still graze my infant head: it's that near. I remember how once, eight candy bananas filled my palm completely. Nowadays, it must be twenty or so, but I wanted to check.

It's interesting, artificial banana. I learned when I was older how the flavor comes from a real, different species of banana, though that one is dead now, webbed in the ramifications of colonization and disease. It's so easy for fungi to prevail in a field of cultivated clones, replicas of biological vulnerability. The microbe which figured out one figured out them all, and now we talk to that ghost-fruit through the static line of candy.

Or at least, I do. Now you're doing it too, with me, if you're reading this.

So I pulled up into the driveway, exactly where the light was slanting, so I could see at least one line, and the blurry figure of a man inside. I tried to remember it, this place. But I couldn't, not really. I could only remember the fact that I had been there.

So I went inside and I asked that man about the banana candy. I figured I'd just get a pack and get back on the road, for old time's sake. I told him it was for old time's sake so I didn't seem too weird to him, asking for candy in the middle of the night, a grown man like me, but the longer I stared at him the more I felt he looked familiar, and then finally he blinked, and when his eyes disappeared and re-emerged, I realized they were the shape of fishbowls.

Even then, I wasn't disturbed. I figured this was one of my therapist's unconventional methods, as I mentioned earlier, and yes, mummy, I know I should've had my suspicions — but I trusted that man. I even trusted him when he pointed to the back of the store, where there were stairs leading upwards into a fluorescent light, and told me they were right up there.

He was sparkling, blue eyes. I felt honored at the time, but now I think it was the look of success more than interest, a string of his self-satisfaction hinged around the thumbtack of my neck.

I do not know why he wanted to capture me. I was walking up these steps, expecting the next perpendicular turn to lead me to another floor, and then the next, and then the next. Eventually I felt I was going insane – I must've been caught in a time loop, repeating the same rounds again, because each step looked exactly like the one before it, and the one before that, though at some point they had stopped leading me upwards. I couldn't find out where the uselessness had begun, where the stairs had stopped being stairs.

Around the hundredth set of steps I began thinking of Baudrillard – yes, pappa, I know this will bore you – and how there is a method to an object leaving reality, which is sort of like the mathematics of death. I can best represent it with the banana candy, which is the essence of a banana which had once existed, which now has become nothing but a flavor, so that when one thinks of its life they imagine only the nostalgic sweetness, and skid neatly past its death.

Now, not only has the banana died, but it has also never lived.

That is how I felt walking up those stairs – which was how I felt when I spoke, how I felt in my room, how I felt in this country, how I feel now, writing this, at the endless top of the world. Each set of stairs became a more impossible thing, a replica of the next, and behind me I began to imagine a fungi crawling upwards, killing neatly as I rose.

In the first days, when you were deciding where to plant me, I remember you took me to a lighthouse. We had stopped at the beach – I was still young. You wiped the sand from the corner of my lips and we scaled the steps and I spread my arms like wings to the wide wide sea. You both laughed and took pictures with the salt-grain lenses. The lighthouse tour guide let us put little notes in bottles and throw them out to sea. I couldn't write yet, so you let me draw a picture. I think I drew a fish, or the idea of a fish, a picture of a picture of a fish: a triangle affixed to a circle. We threw it together. It's still swimming out there, with the rest of them.

If I'm right, that's where I've ended up. I'm heading there now, that window at the top, and there'll be an ocean below me. I already hear the cold roar.

The candy will be there too. I'll figure out how many bananas fit in my palms. If you read this, send your guesses.

Imagine the size of my hands, and keep me alive.

Take care,
Subrayan.

The Service Station Between Thoughts

by Madeleine Swann

Last Tuesday, as I waited in the hallway to go into my Solicitor's Qualifying Examination, I made an impromptu visit to the Service Station in between thoughts about whether I might fail my exam and the Twix I had last night. I was immediately charmed by the attentive staff – only three heads that day – who provided us with maps on arrival.

My first visit was to the rock pool. The rocks themselves were every colour you could think of, and some you couldn't. My favourite was the mini volcano and I wondered which of us had conjured it into existence. My immediate guess was the buttoned-up lady with the glasses but I've learned you can never be sure of these things.

I pointed out my rock to the others – a beautiful turquoise – but the interest was mainly mine. They were more invested in the things frolicking among them, namely several tiny mermaids and a number of suited businessfolk discussing "the grind." It was exhausting just to listen to them, and I was certain they'd have an impossible job "living that boss mindset" out in such remote surroundings, so I didn't stay long.

Out in the fields, which were purple this time, was a centaur teaching archery and, beyond that, a hike through the Bubblegum trees to see the chick of a parasitic lawyer. The egg had been laid in the nest of a construction worker and he had thrown his "siblings" out in order to keep the worms for himself. You could hear him below, arguing to himself again and again, all the reasons why it had been necessary to do such a thing, as though trying to convince himself he had been within his rights. I'd been a bit concerned I would see the construction chick corpses but, luckily, they'd been consumed by something already.

Back in the field, I stuck my head through a swirling vortex, the plaque beside it reading "travel through time and space to worlds unimaginable."

This time I peered through the ceiling of a couple in Maidstone having a passive-aggressive conversation about the amount of coke cans building up on his bedside table. I'd tried the vortex before and it was an improvement on last time, when all I'd seen was my back leaning into the vortex.

After a few other fun diversions – such as the sideshow stage where a mermaid with a fish head tap danced and a pink elephant screamed about being so tired because all it wanted to do was go home but it couldn't as long as everyone kept thinking about it, and couldn't people just forget about it for five minutes so it could get some shut-eye – I was snapped back to reality by my lecturer announcing it was time to head in for the exam. I was tempted to tell my companions about the place but didn't want to deal with the increase in visitors, and thus a potentially less unified place, and I thank goodness that this review page is hidden behind a password.

Ten Detours with You

by Brian Ferguson-Avery

1. Karasek Planetarium, Rosemont, Washington

The mistake was stopping off at the gift shop before-hand. Among the postcards and t-shirts was a basket of brownies. A hand-lettered sign read, "ONE PER CUSTOMER PLEASE." You had to ask why, and the clerk behind the counter said, "They are very popular. A local baker supplies them."

You winked at her. She frowned, confused, blinking back. When you asked for ingredients, she didn't know. "Just usual brownie ingredients, I guess." And you winked again. "Maybe something that's locally grown?" She grew flustered at your insinuations — she may have even thought you were hitting on her. You leaned into me and whispered, "Buy one for me too."

By the time we tilted back into the viewing seats, you couldn't stop the giggles. The one bite you shared with me had caused me to feel nothing strange. Yet you insisted they were hitting you hard. The lights went down, the stars came out upon the ceiling, and you laughed. When the host used his laser light to point out Orion and his belt, a super-imposed rendering of the hunter appeared over the constellation. "He's a hottie!" you smacked. Sagittarius held his bow, and you made "Pew! Pew!" shooting sounds. The bear, the bull, the lion — you provided animal noises. You had a harder time with Libra's scale. But you made a pretty good imitation of Cygnus, though I think it might have been more goose than swan. By then, you were cackling outright. Finally, with Virgo, you shouted, "It's been so long, I forget what one sounds like!" The auditorium doors opened and a uniformed guard ushered us out. On our way out the exit, you called, "Can I get another brownie?"

2. Arrow Mark County Prison, Arrow Mark, Wyoming

In that frontier town, you thought this tour would be a distraction from hours of driving. Housing

convicts until the 1920s, the old prison now sported
peeling paint alongside its bars and rusted metal
bunks. More recently, Fritz Films had come in
to make a horror movie. The crew had torn out a
fifteen-foot section of the prison wall, promising
to rebuild it after they were done shooting. But the
movie flopped, the production company went bank-
rupt, and the wall was never rebuilt.

You gripped my hand, holding us back from
the group. "This way." And you stepped through the
opening in the wall, out into a landscape of scrub
brush and sage. I looked both ways; beyond the wall
appeared more forlorn than the dusty yard inside.
You had me hold the barbed wire apart as you led us
through vacant lots. But you beamed the whole time,
holding your arms wide. "We escaped! Breathe the
free air!"

3. Freas Fossil Pit, David County, Wisconsin

This one wasn't your fault. We started down the trail,
hiking on an early spring day. The bugs weren't out
yet. I took off my sweatshirt and tied it around my

waist, and we stopped to pick bluebells. We were looking forward to digging for some brachiopods.

First, we heard the sirens. You stood in the road to gawk at the helicopter overhead, and you didn't see the patrol car speeding our way; I pulled you from its path just in time. Others followed with flashing lights, and one of them announced over its loudspeaker, "Turn back! Police!" You assured me it didn't pertain to us, so we continued down the road. And then we met the K-9 cops. You would have petted the dogs, but the officers held us back, in their tactical gear and helmets. There was no confusion this time; they told us to leave the area.

"But we wanted to look for fossils!" you said.

"You need to turn back," one of the cops said. The dogs were straining at their leads.

"It's a criminal on the loose, isn't it?" You were gleeful in possibilities. "A drug dealer? A murderer?"

They didn't answer, and you weren't disappointed that we missed the chance to look for petrified shells. You speculated all the way back on who it might have been.

4. The Salt House, Johnson, Virginia

In the 1700s, the settlers employed what is called
the open-pan method to produce salt for flavoring
and food preservation. This museum, an old house
in need of repair, with a few displays, was staffed by
a handful of high-school students on summer break.
One of the kids led us around to explain the process.
He spoke in such a rout recitation, having repeated
the spiel for tourists so many times, that you started
to yawn. Wooden pans, old buckets, corroded ladles
that had been unearthed in archaeological digs –
you finally interrupted the sing-song presentation.
"What's behind that door?"

He stopped and frowned. "That door?" Painted
white and no taller than us, it was marked with a
crisscross of red danger tape.

You started towards it and even tried the old
glass knob. Locked.

"It's being renovated," the teen guide said.

"But what's behind it? Can we take a look? I
promise I won't go in. I just want to see."

He was unable to tell us, beyond some basic
facts about the room being the old pantry.

"But what's it look like?"

When he tried to return to his prepared script, you said, "I don't need to hear about the family again. You already told us that. Don't you have the key to the room?"

No one in the house did, and so we left. I had the feeling that the teenage guide would have a hard time restarting any tours that day.

5. Glass Museum, Stodge, Connecticut

I never learned what drew you to these places. This was a small house that had been filled with shelves and cases to display row upon row of antique bottles, vases, and drinking vessels. We parked next to the three dark SUVs; we didn't notice the diplomatic plates until later. Two swarthy men in suits flanked the front door. I held back, but you said, "Screw them!" and walked right past. They must have signaled to others inside that you were trouble. In a couple minutes — just enough time to pay the entrance fee and read the information in the first display case — they escorted us outside.

The museum's vice president came out to apologize. He explained that an Iranian minister had a meeting at a nearby university. He pronounced the diplomat's name — "Reza Noubary" — as if we should have recognized it. The minister's wife had come to the museum and was inside, pleasantly observing without comment. The vice president asked if we wanted to visit on a later date. He stood with us in the parking lot — glad for the chance to smoke — until we climbed back into our car and pulled away. The guards kept their stern watch from the porch.

6. Middlebourne Cathedral, England

For a small city, the cathedral was massive. Kings and duchesses and priests and all manner of ordinary sinners had traipsed over the flagstones for the past seven centuries, and nearly every surface held a record of their passage. Words had been carved in the chapel lintel, brass plaques punctuated the floor, and long eulogies scrolled in marble on every tomb. "So much information!" you exclaimed. You stopped to read each item, every single line of dedication, each place and date. "Seventeen monks are buried

here — dead from the plague. And who was this
Guinevere Kile? Here, look — this baby was born in
India and died when she was... How old is that?"

I warned you it was getting late, and several
members of the staff had to ask us to leave. "I
haven't seen everything," you shouted, but I think
it was so you could hear your voice echo from the
narthex.

7. The Mystery, outside Rythian, Arizona

For miles and miles along the highway, signs piqued
your interest. "VISIT THE MYSTERY!" "YOU
WON'T BELIEVE THE MYSTERY!" "THE MYS-
TERY! ONLY 31 MORE MILES!" This tourist trap
was stuffed into a menagerie of conjoined buildings,
and there seemed little sense in what it displayed.
Antique cars, army uniforms, a collection of oddly
shaped apples preserved in specimen jars, hair
sculptures in frames. "Rejects from Ripley's," you
said. Signs in each doorway and arrows painted on
the floor kept summoning us towards The Mystery,
which was set off in its own room near the end of
the tour. But right before we stepped through the
curtain, you said, "I need to go back." I followed,

returning past the stuffed buffalo, the collection of metates and telegraph receivers, the row of dinosaur femurs. You were the first to crawl under the turnstile, and when I balked, you tugged my hand.

"We paid for this," I said. "Can't you let me go in and finish?"

"Come on back to the car," you said.

The woman at the ticket booth smacked her gum. "Are you okay, sweetie?"

"I'm fine," you said. "I didn't want to see it."

"Too spooky for you? It's really not that spooky."

"Oh, I've seen spooky shit," you assured her. "This isn't spooky."

"We can't refund your money," she said, looking over at me.

With a straight face, you explained, "No problem. I just knew that whatever is in there, I'm going to be disappointed."

8. Susquehanna House of Wax, New Damascus, Pennsylvania

By "spooky shit," I knew you meant the wax museum. But I couldn't figure what it was that scared you, because nothing in this place seemed very convincing. The figures looked fake, with badly bunched hair and poreless mannikin skin. Sometimes their eyes didn't point right and their shoulders hunched or sat crookedly. Their clothes were polyester. The ground in each diorama was flat and covered by astroturf. The museum purported to illuminate the history of the area, with recorded voices and effects piped in from speakers barely hidden behind rocks and butter churns. You didn't like the diseased children shown from the cholera epidemic, or the militia skirmishes from forgotten battles.

"I think we should get you out of here," I said.

But you persisted. The worst was the Indian attack on white settlers. Two colonists beat a prone Native American with a club. A wide-eyed woman had fallen on the floor from an errant bullet. Cellophane flames rose from the roof, amid screams and gunshots. A man leaned in the corner, an arrow in his gut, and a mechanism inside pumped his chest in desperate gasps. Your grip on my arm grew so firm that I later found bruises shaped by your fingertips. I pulled you out the emergency exit.

For the next two weeks, I'd ask if you wanted to talk about it. You told me to shut up, as you tossed and turned and kept us both awake. When you did fall asleep, you'd wake me up, striking me with your thrashing arms.

9. Shecktor Adobe House, Andrews, California

You kept misreading the word as "abode." "The *abode* house? Isn't that like calling it a *'house* house'?" I laughed along, thinking you were having fun, but you actually had misread it. And then, once I told you it was *adobe*, you said you'd never heard of it. "Mud? A house made of mud?" The docent overheard us and began to relate how the wildfires five years before had burned the parts of the original house that were wood, though the adobe walls remained standing. "Mud doesn't burn," said the docent.

"I was just going to say that!" you chirped.

The gardens outside featured native plants. A warning about a rattlesnake had been posted, mainly to keep kids and pets away. From the shade of the porch, the docent told us to be cautious, to leave it alone if we spotted it.

This time, it was me who said, "Let's go."

But you had already crossed the yard. "I want to see the snake!" You picked up a stick and poked under the arms of the desert sumac.

"Ma'am," called the docent. "I wouldn't do that."

I told you I was leaving.

You stood up. "You're just going to leave me here?"

I held up the keys to the rental car. "We're late for our reservation. The others are waiting."

"Just a minute," and you headed farther down the path, scouting under each bush and cactus.

It's a good thing you got into the passenger seat, just as I was pulling out of the parking lot. I think I was ready to leave you right then.

10. Marino Caverns, Kentucky
In the gift shop, you gawked at the rubber tomahawks and told the boy he shouldn't buy these because they were murder weapons. You purred the word out in psychopathic pleasure:

"Murrrr-derrrrrr..." He backed off and ran to his parents, who gave us dirty looks.

I thought that would be the thing that would get us kicked out. You went to the ticket taker, engaged in an animated conversation. You pointed to yourself, to me, to the glowering parents and red-eyed child, and then to everyone in the room. A while later, you came over. I thought you would say it was time for us to leave.

Instead, it was, "Our turn for the tour. Let's go." And you led me down the metal steps into the cavern at our appointed time. The underground air was chilly and damp, with a smell of musty earth. The stalactites were behind a wire screen, protecting the thousand-year-old formations from careless hands. Still, someone had managed to push candy wrappers through the mesh.

You stopped and pulled my hand. "Wait." We stood in the center of the underground room, and then, after half a minute, the lights went out.

The blackness was infinite. My eyes tried to adjust, but there was nothing beyond sight for them to see. I could not tell if my eyes were open – if I was looking at the dark, seeing the dark — or if my sight was simply shut off. I strained for something that was not there, an ache in my head, like muscles reaching for something just beyond.

But you were there, and I could hear you beside me. You were also breathing quickly, but not from panic. With you, it was excitement. I could smell the whiff of what you'd showered with that morning, and the tang of your hair along the back of your neck opened like a petal. My heart beat under your palm.

I'd been reaching for my phone, to bring a tiny slip of light to the ink. But you stayed my hand.

Your whisper was a giant in the dark. "Don't worry. This was my doing. We'll stay here as long as you like."

Move Up Day

by Aliya Tene'

Bebe stood in front of the painting for a long time. She stood too close though, and for too long, and several times other visitors were forced to say, "excuse me," or ask her to step back a little so they could view the painting as well. Set on a mixed peach and brown and mauve backdrop, three deep walnut figures formed a line down the center of the work. An old woman with silver hair weaved an intricate quilt at the bottom of the line. Just behind her, a small child worked through the grandmother's white tresses with a comb. And just behind the child, sat a woman, elbows up, cornrowing the little girl's hair.

That was all anybody noticed, the three generations of women focused so earnestly on their weaving and braiding and, in that way, on loving each other. That's what they said. That's what they thought, these random onlookers and their rudimentary – if not errant – analyses. Bebe could hear

them. That was all they talked about. They only saw
the women, Bebe thought, and missed so many of
the most important parts. Did they not see the tree
of life? The man in the white hat? The faces of the
lost? The ancestors? The fish? The owl? The dog?
The three original spellcasters in their healing circle?
The teeth of the devil? Nissa's face – her beautiful
face – sitting right there at Mom's elbow? Couldn't
they see any of it?

Bebe stood there studying the painting so long
that a museum docent asked her if she didn't want
to see the other works in the exhibit along with her
schoolmates.

Bebe did not.

The docent was wearing a purple name tag that
read "Betty" with "AAMP" in large white letters
stacked on top of each other like the red letters on
the LOVE statue in Love Park.

"Your class has already gone up to the next
level," the lady said to Bebe, twisting her painted
coral lips together upon finishing her statement. The
woman was troublingly thin and very light skinned.
Green and blue veins shot through her hands and

showed at her temples. If it weren't for something about her, her cheekbones maybe, maybe her nose, she would almost pass for white. Her grey and white streaked hair, which was pulled back and fashioned into an efficient, color coordinated clip-in bun, was straight and fine and so thin that Bebe could see her scalp peeking through the wefts.

This lady don't know nothin' about getting cornrows, Bebe thought.

Bebe remembered getting her own hair corn-rowed when she was small and how much it hurt. Her father had allowed her mother to do "straight backs" just like the child's hair in the painting. All the boys were getting straight backs then anyway. But when Bebe had asked for pink and gold beads on the ends like Nissa's, and her mother went to pick up a pink bead, her father had raised his open hand.

Her mother and grandmother and Nissa had gone into the parlor that night and closed Bebe out. The white hat was still in Bebe's mother's bedroom closet, but that was the last time she'd seen her dad.

"Your class is just being seated for the short informative documentary on the collection. Just this way," the docent said to her. And then, like a game show vixen showing off a brand-new car, she forced her overdrawn lips into a toothy white-capped smile and gracefully waved her scrawny arm to her side, indicating the nearby ramp to the third level of the exhibit. The lady nodded at Bebe. "If you would," she said.

Bebe would not.

Above the docent's head, scripted marigold letters danced across a slate blue screen: "Unsigned, Anonymous, and Lost," they said. In the next frame was an outline of the African continent with the subtitle: "Found and Salvaged Creative Works by Unnamed Children of the Diaspora." The docent turned to see what Bebe was looking at and revealed a sculpture that had been sitting on the wall shelf just behind her. It was made of dark wood that had been shined and polished to a glossy finish. The carved piece presented an elongated face, which appeared bald on the top of its head, with enormous, outsized lips, a chunky nose, and a perfect set of long burnt umber teeth. The sculpture seemed folded and wrinkled above the eyebrows, and had tufts of coarse hair protruding above the ears, creating the distorted visage of a very old man. And even though he appeared to be smiling broadly, something about the image was distinctly unhappy. Or, thought Bebe, it was happy for all the wrong reasons. Whoever made that, she thought, they're not right.

Then she turned back to the painting.

"If you don't know who made them, if they are anonymous, how do you know they are children of the diaspora?"

"Well..." the docent was nonplussed by the question. *All of the information was in the video presentation. If this... this... PERSON would just go and watch the damned video...*

"The subject usually, of course," she continued out loud. "Artists rarely create people who don't look like themselves, do they? But we have researchers who find out all they can about the pieces. It's all in the video playing upstairs if you're ready to go watch it now."

"If you don't know who made them, how do you know why they were left behind or thrown away? What if there was a reason?"

"Well, art should never be thrown away," the docent replied. "All art has a purpose."

"What if the purpose isn't good?" Bebe said, her eyes returning to the sculpture. She knew what it was without moving any closer and that the person who had created it had not looked anything like the image. Bebe could feel the thing, could not stand to move any closer to it than she already was. It was the likeness of a betrayer, laughing at the downfall of someone like him, someone who trusted him. Whoever had carved it had filled it with angry and jealous energy. It was hateful. She stopped looking at it and turned back to the peach mauve painting.

"Well, who are we to say?" the docent said.

Bebe didn't answer.

Well, somebody better say, Bebe thought. But she knew it wouldn't be her. She had worked hard to hide the things she knew, and the things she was beginning to be able to do. Bebe realized early on that people very much wanted to keep their private thoughts private, and she didn't blame them. When her abilities had first started after Nissa died, she thought she could only do it sometimes, off and on, like a fluke. Later, she realized she could always read a person's thoughts or feelings if she tried, but most of the time she didn't try.

Some people, though, like this museum volunteer, thought so loudly that Bebe couldn't shut her out. She was like Bebe's own grandmother in that way. People like this lady and Bebe's grandmother, and Bebe's father for that matter, whose own thoughts were so amplified, listened to the views of others only to the extent that they mirrored their own. This lady could only understand the things she already believed anyway. She could never comprehend how Bebe knew that the sculpture on the wall behind her was one they should have just left among the lost.

The woman was still trying her best to be polite and professional, but Bebe knew the old lady had become annoyed with her. She was annoyed that Bebe wasn't moving with her class, that she was blocking the view for other patrons, that she was *outside of the proper school group tour protocols and procedures*. And, Bebe knew, this old lady was most annoyed that she didn't know what to make of Bebe.

She was trying to figure out if Bebe was a girl or a boy; was even more indignant that she should be *forced* to be so confused because in her day *people looked like what they were, and a person could tell a young man from a young woman. Even if the boy was funny actin, you could still tell that he was a boy...* In her day, the lady thought. And Bebe heard all of it. More correctly, she felt all of it, but she heard some of the words quite directly. All the confused and hateful things old Betty Jean was thinking, Bebe knew them – felt them hitting her like tiny needles pricking the back of her head... But she still couldn't move away.

She reached out to touch the painting, but quickly drew her hand back. What if this wasn't it? It was wrong, after all. Maybe not wrong exactly, but it was different, anyway, than she remembered it. It had been a few years since her mother had gone into a rage and tossed the painting off the front porch down to the heap of trash sitting on the sidewalk. Maybe Bebe's memory of the painting wasn't perfect, she allowed, but something did seem different about it now. She knew that. It had changed. It had changed, but it was still the same.

It was like seeing a friend from first grade again after going off to high school. Like Aaron. When Bebe had seen Aaron, her best friend from her first elementary school, in the McDonald's on Broad Street last month, she had been so happy to see him that she squealed and hugged him tight, squeezing his whole body and pinning his arms into the hug. Perhaps that was why Bebe hadn't immediately noticed that Aaron never raised his arms to hug her back. He pulled away from her, in fact, looked her up and down and said, "You... you're, umm, you're different." But so was he. They were both the same people they had always been really, but different.

So, it *could be* the painting, right? Just different? And what if it was? She had to feel it. She had to feel the work against her own living skin to be sure this was it... to trace the edges of the painted tree with her fingertip, to feel where the acrylic was thick and gnarled like old bark, to lay her palm against the softness of the growing quilt, to smooth the loose downy strands of the grandmother's hair. She had to *feel* it to know if this was really it.

The docent had walked across the room to address a newly arriving group, but she'd kept her eyes on Bebe.

"Please don't touch the exhibits. The oils in a person's hand could ruin..." The docent, glaring at Bebe over her red framed glasses, had begun to shout and point in Bebe's direction. But that was as far as she had gotten. Bebe was already reaching her long slender arm out over the red velvet rope to find her answers.

As soon as she pressed the tips of her fingers to the painting, a feeling like hot water, as soothing as a bath but somehow as vast and measureless as the sea, flowed through her entire body. The mighty swell started small in the tips of her fingers but soon grew into a wave, warming her to her soul, and Bebe received everything the painting meant to give. It was Love. It was magic, there was no doubt. It was immense power and divination. It was legacy and history and blood and sorrow. It was protection and connection — to her family — to the ancestors — to the earth — to the Creator. It was an immovable constant. It was boundless growth. It was understanding and change and the heat of the sun. But, more than anything, it was Love.

And then it was Nissa, standing before Bebe in the peach mauve light of the painting with the tree and the ancestors, and the animals, and the dangers, and the spellcasters blurring all around them.

"It's you, Sister," Nissa said. "I am here. I am always here for you. But it is you." She kissed Bebe three times on her forehead. Then she faded back into the peaches and pinks and browns, and everything was gone. Bebe was standing before the painting again on the proper side of the velvet rope.

When Bebe drew her arm back and looked around, she saw that the docent and the other visitors were standing completely still. They had not moved. The docent's mouth was open, her arm raised and finger pointing. Some of the crowd was looking at Bebe. Some were not. One little boy had been removing his zipped jacket over his head and was stuck in mid-takeoff. The display screen on the wall was trapped in a transition between the last image and the next. Everything around her was frozen. And, across the room, the burnt carving of the betrayer was split right down the middle.

It's me, Bebe said to herself. I did this. I'm holding them all in place. And then she remembered Nissa's kisses. It's me, she said to herself again, this time smiling. I did this.

And, thinking of the Mauve, she blew a kiss into the air and set them all free.

***

"Mom?" Bebe sat at the dining room table, using one French fry to push the others around her plate.

"Be?" Bebe's mom never called her Bebe. Never once. She had stopped calling her Brandon when Bebe was six and had outright refused to respond to it, but "Be" was as far as she ever got.

"Remember that painting that used to be in the parlor?'

"No."

"Yes, you do, Mom. Remember it had a grand-mom at the top, and then a younger lady in the middle, and then a little girl, and they were all braiding each other's hair?"

Leave it to Be to bring up this shit, Bebe's mom thought. And Bebe heard it.

"I... I just bring it up because, that's the order, right? The grandmom at the top, then the mom, then the little daughter?"

"Yes, Be. That's how it was."

Bebe's mom didn't want to talk about the painting. It was supposed to be a family heirloom, a record. It was supposed to stay with the women in their family forever, harnessing their magic, warning them of danger, illuminating needed spells, designating and revealing the order and hierarchy of their power, and reminding them of their legacy. But their family's magical lineage had been ripped away when her oldest daughter, Nissa, was killed in a car accident. And all that painting could do in the days after that was remind Bebe's mom of the deepest sorrow on the earth, and the worst time in all of their lives.

"She was the last of us," Bebe's grandmother had said to her mother at Nissa's repast. It wasn't the official repast where everyone goes after the service and has bland church chicken and diabetes flavored juice. It was the after-repast repast, when it's just the family and a few best friends, and the people left eat too much cake, and drink too much beer, and slip out of their good but painful shoes.

"It's got to be three." Bebe's grandmother was sitting next to her mother on the couch in the parlor looking up at the painting. "It's got to be three in a line. That's how it's always been. But when the last goes first…" She shook her head, her silvery pressed curls now fallen from a hard day's challenge and dangling in her face. "Well, we'll follow shortly after, you and I. If not in the flesh, then in the spirit. You may as well toss that painting into the fireplace," she had said. "Our magic will be fading soon."

"What about Be? There's still three with Be."

"Shut up what you talkin'," Bebe's grandmother had snapped. Her whisper was sharper than any-body's holler. "This is woman's magic. That's how it passes. Through the women. Born women."

"I know it's 'woman's magic,' Mama, but, Be is…"

Bebe's grandmother had stood up then, tower-ing over her mourning hopeful daughter, her face contorted in frustration.

"It's what I say," she said. "You raised them children how you thought best. So, that's on you. Be is what Be is. But Be also ain't what she ain't. You hear me? It's what I say. Watch our magic. It will be fading soon. See if it don't. And get rid of that painting. If we ain't three, we can't practice. We broke the line. It ain't meant for us no more. It don't serve us no more. And we don't keep what don't serve. Toss it right into the fire."

Bebe's mother had not tossed the painting into any fire, but two days later, in her own grief and anger, she had yanked the painting down off the wall, kicked the thick wooden frame into three pieces with the canvas still clinging by its staples, and chucked the heavy painting – more correctly, flung it, like it was as light as a spitball, without touching it at all – up over the front stairs and slammed it down on top of the heap of bags siting at the curb awaiting that morning's pickup. She had done what her mother had told her to; gotten rid of it. And, just as she was warned would happen, after a while, she had noticed Bebe's grandmother's magic begin to fade. But her own magic...

***

"I saw it today," Bebe said, looking down at the fries and not at her mother. "I touched it and everything."

"No, you didn't."

"I know you threw it away, but I saw it at the museum today. On our school trip. I saw it."

"What museum?"

"The Black one."

Bebe's mom sighed. "At the African American Museum of Philadelphia? Those fancy ass museum people go around picking stuff out of the trash, now? No, you didn't see our painting there. That painting is long gone. And good riddance. It wasn't meant for us anymore."

"Well, I thought I saw it," Bebe said. "But the grandmom was at the bottom making a quilt instead of at the top braiding hair."

Bebe's mom gripped her by the cheeks and swirled Bebe around in her chair to face her. "What did you say?"

"I said..."

"I know what you said, Be. I heard you! I just want you... Just..." She let go, sat down in the chair next to Bebe's own and took a deep breath. "Be, just tell me exactly what you saw. Tell me everything you saw, everything you did... And say it slow."

When Bebe had finished the telling, her mom dropped her head into her own hands and cried.

"I didn't think it was you," she said. "I thought our power was lost when Nissa... I thought you had to be... I'm so sorry, Be. I'm so sorry... Bebe."

Bebe grabbed her mother's tear-streaked face then, and lifted it upwards to look at her own. "No, Mom. You always knew who I was. You and Nissa. You let them tell you different, make you believe different, but you knew. You always knew me."

Bebe's mom hugged her then, held her as tightly as she could, in the way that all good moms do when they are willing all the love and healing inside them into their daughters.

"I threw our legacy away," Bebe's mom said after a while. "Tossed it out with the garbage, and now it's stuck in a museum... like a fossil." She shook her head at herself, grieving all her past mistakes. "We'll never get it back."

Bebe looked at her, a little surprised, then threw a cold French fry up in the air, blew a kiss, and froze it in place. Her mother's jaw dropped as it hung in the air in front of her, and Bebe smiled.

"I don't think we'll have a problem bringing it home," Bebe said.

Review: The Last Good Diner on the Road to the End of the World

by Brittany Thomas

They serve eggs any way out here if you ask nicely. Black coffee with free refills, creamer in little pods on the table. It smells like home fries and bacon and a Monte Cristo soaking in maple syrup. They've got a Reuben on rye stacked high the New York way. The waitress comes by again with the coffee pot. There's a dumpster fire out back that no one mentions; twelve cars piled up on the curb on a carpet of broken glass. There's a cloche full of fluffy donuts on the counter — they're covered in sugar and filled with jam. Yes, they might be able to find you an herbal tea (in a box that expired in 2003, it's fine). The Western omelette is big enough for three people and they serve it with a steak knife. Another refill? They're free. The sirens are louder now. Buffalo chicken on a hard roll. Turkey club — white, wheat or rye — with a long wedge of dill pickle hidden under twice cooked fries. Award-winning regional chowder: cup or bowl served with a little packet of oyster crackers. A wiry dog paces in the parking lot, waiting for his turn. Someone moves a body from the doorway. It's a long way to the end of the world, might as well try the Very Veggie Skillet. Someone named Barbara named at least two of the breakfast sandwiches. Country hash, garbage plate, French toast stuffed with bananas, an anxiety of muffin varieties. What's that? Time to go? Another lost soul needs my seat at the counter, good luck out there. They'll do your eggs any way you like.

Meet the Authors

M. Lopes da Silva (he/they/she) is a white Latinx and non-binary trans masc author, artist, and critic from Los Angeles. He writes pulp and poetry. Dread Stone Press recently published his first novelette *What Ate the Angels* — a queer vore sludgefest that travels beneath the streets of Los Angeles starring a non-binary ASMR artist and their vore-loving girl-friend — in Volume Two of the *Split Scream* series.

Bitter Karella is the writer and horror aficionado behind the microfiction comedy account @Midnight__pals, which asks what if all your favorite horror writers gathered around the campfire to tell scary stories. When not writing twitter jokes, he also dabbles in cartooning and text game design.

Corey Farrenkopf lives on Cape Cod with his wife, Gabrielle, and works as a librarian. His short stories have been published in Three-Lobed Burning Eye,

SmokeLong Quarterly, Uncharted, Catapult, The Southwest Review, Reckoning, Flash Fiction Online, Bourbon Penn, and elsewhere. To learn more, follow him on Twitter @CoreyFarrenkopf or on the web at CoreyFarrenkopf.com

Nicole M. Wolverton is a Pushcart-nominated writer living in the Philadelphia, Pennsylvania area. Her debut YA horror novel *A Misfortune of Lake Monsters* is forthcoming in 2024 (CamCat Books); she is also the author of the adult thriller *The Trajectory of Dreams* (Bitingduck Press, 2013) and editor of *Bodies Full of Burning*, an anthology of short horror fiction (Sliced Up Press, 2021). Her short stories and creative nonfiction have appeared in dozens of publications.

DeBussy O'Slamahain is a transgender man (he/him) with a Creative Writing degree from Bloomsburg University, a loving fiancé, many furry and scaly children, and a heart full of dread and wonder. Hydrate yourself dear reader and have mercy on yourself.

Dewi Hargreaves is a writer and illustrator from the cold, soggy middle of the UK. His short fiction has appeared in publications by Etherea Magazine, Magic and Moons Press and Noctivagant Press, amongst others. His flash fiction story 'Maccabeus' came 2nd in Grindstone Literary's Open Prose Competition 2017. He has self-published two books, *The Shield Road* and *Eyes on the Blue Star*.

Harley Showers: Fiction writer in the genres of fantasy, horror, and humor. Indulges in far too-much media as long as it isn't social. Is an avid content creator on Twitch and WordPress and plays roleplaying games in his free time.

Steve Novak is an ordinary working man with a passion of story. His first writings were non-fiction, but he's since seen the light. His first published fiction is the story "You Give Me Fever" in the anthology *Island Fever*. He's currently querying his first novel.

Devaki Devay is an Indian writer of fiction, poetry, and creative non-fiction. Their work can be found at Barren Magazine and Peatsmoke journal! Follow them @DevakiDevay on Twitter.

Madeleine Swann's collection, *The Sharp End of the Rainbow*, was published by Heads Dance Press and her novella, *The Vine That Ate The Starlet*, was released by Filthy Loot.

Her novella, *Fortune Box* (Eraserhead Press), was nominated for a Wonderland Award. Her short stories have appeared in various anthologies and podcasts including Splatterpunk Award nominated *The New Flesh: A David Cronenberg Tribute*.

Brian Ferguson-Avery is a writer who loves any visitor center that isn't closed. He buys cheap postcards from their gift shops and sends them to friends, and plans someday to wallpaper his room with the postcards that friends have sent him. His short-story collection, *Rough Jointed Beasts*, was recently published by Feral Indie Studio, and he has had stories, poems, and essays published in places such as *JAMA*, *Crossings*, *Quarterly West*, *Rosebud*, and *Short Story*.

Aliya Tene' is a word-a-phile who started writing poems in elementary school and who, over the years, has followed the muse into writing everything from plays, to music, to screenplays, to short fantastic tales of unruly fae. Right now, she is grateful to be completing her first horror novel – or 2 – as an MFA candidate at Rosemont College. Aliya is an Assistant Professor of English in Philadelphia. She is currently obsessed with the Arrowverse, is suspicious of people who choose mild taco sauce, and has a firm belief that most dogs are better people than actual people, except for those in her own beautiful loving family – of course.

Brittany Thomas is a queer writer who was born and raised in upstate New York and currently lives in London (and misses diners). Her writing appears in *Bullshit Lit*, Fifth Wheel Press's *Come Sail Away* anthology, *JAKE*, *Scrawl Place*, and *The Daily Drunk Magazine*. You can find her on Twitter @britomatic.

Milton Keynes UK
Ingram Content Group UK Ltd.
UKHW020933181223
434584UK00001BA/2

9 798218 256852